Heart's♡Reward

DONNA HILL

Heart's ♥ Reward
A Match Made Novel

ARABESQUE®

Recycling programs
for this product may
not exist in your area.

HEART'S REWARD

ISBN-13: 978-0-373-83183-8

www.kimanipress.com

Printed in U.S.A.

Dear Reader,

We hope you enjoy *Heart's Reward,* the final story in Arabesque's Match Made series. Over the past three months we have introduced you to the Platinum Society—an exclusive matchmaking service run by Melanie Harte, a third-generation matchmaker, for wealthy, high-profile clients.

Never get involved with the client has always been Melanie Harte's motto, and her reputation depends on it. Yet suddenly two of her most eligible prospects are pursuing the matchmaker herself. Rafe Lawson is a senator's son with a player's charm and a seductive smile. Claude Montgomery is the senator's ambitious, charismatic and very attractive special assistant. Both men are off-the-charts sexy—and completely off-limits. But as Melanie's feelings for one of them deepens, it puts more than her company at risk.

We hope you enjoyed the entire Match Made series. And if you missed the first two novels— *Heart's Secret* by Adrianne Byrd and *Heart's Choice* by Celeste O. Norfleet—be sure to read about those couples and how they found their match made in heaven.

Evette Porter
Editor
Arabesque

This book is totally dedicated to my editor
Evette Porter who has the patience of a saint!
Thanks for your support.

Acknowledgment

I want to thank all of the wonderful readers who continue to support my work. You guys are the amazing ones. I could not do this without you. I hope I continue to write the stories that make you feel good.

A big shout out goes to Adrianne Byrd and Celeste O. Norfleet for their amazing work on this series. Both are hard acts to follow.

I hope you enjoy this steamy conclusion to the Match Made series. I had an interesting time writing about Melanie Harte and the dilemmas she finds herself in. I would love to hear what you think about *Heart's Reward* and the entire series. Join my blog, www.donnahill.blogspot.com, and share your thoughts, or send me an e-mail at dhassistant@gmail.com. And you can always visit me online at www.donnahill.com or on Facebook. I'd love to hear from you!

Prologue

The Harte mansion sat majestically on the bluffs of Sag Harbor, overlooking the swell of waves across the bay. The nearest neighbor was a long walk away—a perfect location since it served to shield the many high-powered clients that frequented it from prying eyes. To the average person it was simply a fabulously gorgeous home tucked away in the quaint Long Island resort town. But the Harte family and the clients they served knew otherwise. The mansion was the home of The Platinum Society, the country's most elite and discreet matchmaking service.

Tonight, however, the mansion shone like a beacon. Its glass windows were lit up by the brilliance of crystal chandeliers and the shimmering glow of candlelight. The line of cars obscured the winding driveway and wrapped around to the back of the house. Music from the live band could be heard drifting across the water, gently wafting through the night air.

Melanie Harte moved among her guests with an assured grace. She had hosted more of these soirees than she could count. Her summer gatherings were an opportunity for her clients to meet and mingle and relax and enjoy some of the perks that their huge fee afforded them. They were always lively affairs, and every party was invariably punctuated with at least one surprise. Tonight was no different.

In the midst of all the music and good food, Melanie grabbed the microphone.

"I hope everyone is having a wonderful time tonight." Her sultry voice rang out over the ebb and flow of conversation until it dimmed. All eyes turned in her direction. "You know how much I love these gatherings and a chance to see all of you."

"We love you, Melanie!" someone shouted from the side of the room.

The crowd burst into spontaneous applause.

"I love you back! But I have something we can all shout about." She introduced Sergio, who came up to the mic.

Sergio Alvarez had graced the cover of hundreds

of magazines and women practically fell over themselves to get his attention. But he'd had no luck in
finding a woman who wanted him for who he was
and not the picture on a cover or the size of his wallet.
He'd been referred by a satisfied client and, once
again, The Platinum Society struck gold. Tonight he
announced his engagement to Valencia Martinez,
a professional photographer who was successful
and financially secure in her own right. They made
the perfect couple and Melanie could just see the
headlines when it was announced that Sergio was
officially off the market.

The guests whooped with joy for the happy couple and the band segued to Earth Wind and Fire's
Celebration.

It was nearly 2:00 a.m. by the time the last guest
filed out. Melanie locked the door, kicked off her
shoes and went to join her family in the kitchen.

"We're all crashing here tonight," her nephew
Vincent announced, draping his arm around his wife,
Cherise. Veronica, his sister, and their cousin Jessica
were seated at the table with their heads nestled on
their folded arms.

"Fine with me. You know where your rooms are."
Melanie yawned.

Jessica stood and stretched. "Pretty great about
Sergio and Valencia."

They all hummed their agreement, too tired to

do much else, and began to drift to their rooms murmuring their good nights.

Melanie set the alarm and turned out the lights. From the top of the stairs she looked out at the room that had been filled with happy, eager people searching for and in some cases finding love.

She turned and opened the door to her bedroom. Her work at least for tonight was done. Tomorrow was another full day. She yawned again. She was going to need every wink of sleep she could get.

Chapter 1

Melanie Harte reluctantly stirred from a deep sleep. She'd dreamed of Steven last night and the three beautiful years they'd spent together. It had been nearly a decade since his death. And although the loss did not feel as painful as it once had, a dull, nagging ache still remained. Widowed at the age of twenty-six, the tragedy had taken all the effervescence out of Melanie's naturally bubbly personality like a soda gone flat. Like her mother and her grandmother, Melanie believed in everlasting love and that there was that special someone for everybody. With Steven gone, so was everything that she'd believed in. At least that is what she'd told herself.

So it was her grandmother, who she'd been named after, and her mother, Carolyn, who came to rescue their wounded darling and immersed her in the family business. Melanie was sure it had saved her life or at least saved her from a life of loneliness.

She worked side-by-side with her Gran and her mother, finding the perfect match for those seeking true love. But their clients were not your casual romance seekers. They were the elite, those rare birds who soared in the stratosphere of celebrity, wealth and high society, whose lifestyles, professions and often notoriety actually worked against them when it came to romance. So they turned to The Platinum Society, Melanie Harte and her expert team of matchmakers to find them that special someone—for a very large fee, of course. Her business afforded her the luxurious lifestyle to which she'd grown very comfortable and accustomed to—a mansion on the bluff of the historic African-American enclave of Sag Harbor in New York's Hamptons, a private jet, a new car every year, a yacht, a hefty bank account, entree to premieres, parties and private dinners virtually in every city in the United States and Europe, an extensive wardrobe and friends around the globe.

It was a good life, she mused as she poked her head above the billowy taupe-colored comforter and squinted against the morning sun. Its intensity and beauty reflected across the water and beamed down through the skylight and the floor-to-ceiling windows of her bedroom. A beautiful summer day was on the horizon and Melanie was sure that the beaches, shops and streets would be teeming with tourists and locals out enjoying the day. She realized the temperature had risen considerably overnight as she sat up and planted her feet on the floor beside the bed. She stood and crossed the room to adjust the central air.

Tugging her silk robe around her, she scurried to the bathroom and turned on the bathtub jets for her morning soak.

She had a thriving business, she thought as she poured bath salts and a capful of baby oil into the bath water, a devoted family and more money than she could ever spend. She was happy. Wasn't she?

By the time she emerged from the sanctuary of her bedroom suite, the aroma of fresh-brewed coffee and homemade biscuits tickled her nose. She'd reluctantly hired a personal chef, Evan, after a stellar recommendation from one of her clients. She usually only hired a chef and caterers when she was hosting a party. But she'd come to realize that after the end of a hard day and because she was alone, she rarely ate. And if she did it wasn't anything healthy. As a result, she'd put on a few extra pounds in the past few months. Pounds that she was determined to shed with diet and exercise. Now she had the incentive to use her home gym.

Dressed in a pearl-gray sleeveless silk jersey top and pants, she walked into the kitchen—her three-inch heels clicking against the floor—to greet Evan and have breakfast.

"Good morning, Evan," she said, swiping a flaky biscuit from the plate on the counter.

Evan turned around from the stainless steel commercial-grade oven with a spatula in his hand. "Good morning. I was preparing an omelet for you. Your nieces and nephew are in the dining room."

"They're here already?"

"They arrived about an hour ago. There's fresh fruit on the table. Coffee or tea?"

Melanie grinned. "Tea." She eased alongside of him to see if she could get a peek at the omelet ingredients. His omelets were to die for and so nutritious.

Evan immediately covered the bowl of ingredients. "Let it be a surprise. Go join the family. I'll bring your breakfast shortly."

Melanie made a face and walked away.

Vincent, Veronica and Jessica were seated around the dining table that could expand to seat ten.

"Morning, Aunt Mel," they chorused.

"How is everyone?" Melanie asked as she poured a glass of orange juice.

"Good," Vincent said. "I went over the accounts last night and—"

"I don't know how Cherise stays married to you," Veronica interjected with a mouth full of pineapple slices. "All you do is work."

Vincent glared at his sister. "Trust me, I make sure my wife is very happy."

"Cherise never complains," Jessica said, putting in her two cents. "All of Vincent's work seems to keep Cherise *very* happy."

"You're much too young to understand, Jess," Veronica said. "A woman wants more than things. She wants to be wined, dined and romanced. Right, Aunt Mel?"

"You're absolutely right, Veronica," Melanie agreed. Jessica made a face at her cousin. "But Vince was taught by the best, Grandma Harte. I'm sure he knows how to take care of home." She winked at her nephew.

Evan brought Melanie an overstuffed omelet and set it down in front of her with a flourish.

"Hmm," Melanie uttered in appreciation. "Thank you, Evan."

"Anyone need anything?" he said, looking around the table.

"We're good," Vincent said.

Evan nodded and walked back into the kitchen.

"What's on the agenda for today?" Melanie asked, cutting into her omelet stuffed with mushrooms, bell peppers, spinach, tomatoes and feta cheese.

Jessica, the youngest and the one who was always prepared for any eventuality, pulled out a folder from the leather briefcase that sat at her feet. She placed it on the table and flipped it open.

"And you accuse me of having a type-A personality," Vincent said to his sister, lifting his chin in Jessica's direction. They all shared a laugh.

Jessica ignored the barb. She told him about the latest inquiry from a Wall Street executive who was seriously in the market for a permanent companion.

As the team was reviewing the client's background, the phone rang.

Melanie turned around and plucked the phone from the cradle behind her. "The Platinum Society, Melanie Harte speaking."

"Mel, it's Alan."

"Alan!" she said over a blossoming smile. "I'm going to put you on speakerphone."

"Dad?" Veronica and Vincent chorused.

"Uncle Alan," Jessica added.

"Hey, everybody," he called out.

"Where are you?" Melanie asked.

Alan Harte was a career diplomat in the State Department. He traveled the globe at the behest of the U.S. government. At any given time he could be called upon to travel across continents for weeks or months on end.

"Actually, I just landed at JFK. I'm here in New York for the next few months. Or so they tell me," he added with a chuckle. "Thought I'd come out to the Harbor later today."

"Of course! We'd love to see you. And you're staying here," his younger sister insisted.

"I'll think about it, sis. I'm in New York but it's not a vacation. I'm on the clock. Getting back and forth from the city to Sag Harbor may be a bit much. But I can certainly spend a couple of days there. I miss the kids. And you," he added, his voice warming with affection for his sister. "And…I, uh, have a favor to ask."

"No problem. What is it?"

"We'll talk about it when I get there."

"Can't you give me a hint?"

"Let's just say I may have a client for you."

The Platinum Society was a family-run business that went back two generations. The current Melanie Harte made it three. Since its inception, well before Melanie's birth, the first Melanie Harte was the consummate matchmaker. Legendary among her circle for pairing up just the right people, the first Melanie Harte realized that she could turn what came naturally to her into a business because she was being asked by everyone from college professors to executives to find them that perfect someone. But it was her daughter, Carolyn, who'd graduated with honors from Columbia University with an MBA in marketing and a BA in psychology, who took the mom-and-pop operation to the next level. She taught her daughter everything she knew, but it was Melanie who took the company *platinum*.

Melanie and the team put off discussing the new client, who was so eager to find a mate that he was willing to pay an extra twenty-five thousand dollars in addition to the standard fifty-thousand-dollar fee. That, to Melanie, was a red flag. She was glad they were temporarily putting that assignment on hold.

Meanwhile her nieces and nephew were busy trying to figure out who Alan's client was.

"It's probably some Secret Service guy," Jessica said. "You know they don't have time to find anyone."

"Do they make enough money to afford us?" Vincent asked.

Melanie shot her nephew a look and bit back a smile. One thing she could say about Vincent, he kept his eye on the bottom line.

"I'm sure Alan told them what we require," Melanie said. "But as you all know we can make an exception if the situation warrants it."

"Aunt Mel, the last exception was in 1955 by your grandmother," Jessica stated skeptically. She was the resident historian of The Platinum Society. She knew everything there was to know about TPS from the very first day to the present. She'd catalogued all of Grandma Harte's notes and Aunt Carolyn's floppy disks and created a comprehensive history and profile of the company, complete with successes, failures, marriages and births in a digital archive and Web site that included narratives, photo galleries, videos and podcasts. "But of course the decision is up to you, Aunt Mel," Jessica added.

The trio looked at her and groaned good-naturedly.

"As soon as I can get all the details on our new client, I'll get busy on a profile and run him through the database for potential matches," Veronica said.

"Uncle Alan has some pretty cool friends," Jessica said. "If he's true to form, this assignment may be as much fun as it is lucrative."

Melanie smiled. "I'm sure you're right."

It was nearing two o'clock when the black Range Rover pulled onto the winding driveway of the Sag Harbor mansion. Melanie spotted it from her ground-floor office window. She hopped up from her desk and darted out into the hallway.

"He's here," she yelled, quickly walking toward the door.

Veronica and Vincent emerged from the kitchen. Jessica bounded up the stairs from the indoor gym, a towel draped around her neck.

The smiling quartet stood in the archway as Alan Harte strode toward the door.

The word that always came to mind when describing her older brother was debonair. There was an air of almost old-world movie star power that radiated from the six-foot- three, two-hundred-and-twenty-pound hunk. An impeccable dresser, handsome, intelligent, well-traveled, funny and financially in the black, with a great job—Alan Harte was a single woman's dream come true. But he loved his freedom, which had led to the demise of his marriage. As her former sister-in-law used to say, Alan may have said his vows to her, but he married his job.

"Always good to come home," he said, softly kissing cheeks and hugging his son, who was the spitting image of his father.

Vincent took his father's overnight bag and briefcase, while his sister and cousin hooked their arms possessively through his with Melanie closing ranks.

"How long are you in town?" Veronica asked.

"I'm thinking a month or two, maybe longer. I'll know in about a week."

"Are you going to stay here for a few days at least?" Melanie asked, and with her question she realized how much she'd missed her brother.

Their sister Phyllis—Jessica's mom—died during childbirth and their parents and grandparents had been gone for many years, so it was just the two of them to look after the next generation.

Alan draped his arm around her shoulder. "Actually, I was planning on staying through the weekend."

Everyone cheered in delight.

"I do have a favor, though."

"Sure," Melanie responded.

Alan looked from one expectant face to the other. "I mentioned in my call that I had a potential client for you. Well, there's a private party and reception at the American embassy…"

All eyebrows rose on cue.

"Black tie, invitation only."

"Get to the good part, Uncle Alan."

Alan chuckled. "That's where your new client will be tonight. I thought it would be a great time to meet him, so I finagled invitations for all of you." His voice lowered. His tone turned mockingly serious. "I presume you have something suitable to wear?"

Whoops of laughter echoed around the room.

Alan tossed his head back and laughed. Man, it was good to be home.

Vincent checked his Rolex. "What time do we need to be ready, and uh, can I bring Cherise?"

"I got you covered, son. Call that pretty wife of yours and tell her that the Hartes are partying tonight. A car will be here to pick us up at seven."

All three women's hands immediately reached for their hair at the same time.

"I'll give Leona a call and let her know we'll be at the shop in a half hour," Melanie said quickly. After all, a woman's crowning glory was her hair. She turned to her brother. "With all of the excitement you never told me who our potential client is."

Four sets of eyes landed on Alan. "His name is Claude Montgomery. He's the chief of staff for Senator Lawson."

The doors to the conference room opened and the corridor filled with conversation. Some voices were raised in laughter, and others were low in muted discussions.

Claude loosened his tie. He veered off from the throng of suits that filled the hallway. He checked his watch. A three-hour meeting. Inwardly he groaned. Most of the time had been spent arguing points that had been debated for the past month. Typical Washington politics. He fully understood the frustration of the President and the American people. He was just as frustrated. No one else seemed to mind. It was business as usual on Capitol Hill. He strode down the hall, putting on his game face to deter even the most relentless lobbyist.

"Mr. Montgomery, these papers need your signature," his secretary said, waylaying him. She carried a folder under her arm that bulged. Her smile was sympathetic.

He'd hoped to be able to sneak away under the radar, tie up some loose ends in his office and catch a plane to New York.

She quickened her step to keep up with him. "I know you have a flight to catch. I've tabbed the pages that you need to sign."

They turned left and walked down another corridor lined with doors. Name plates identified the offices. His office was around the next turn. He opened the door and let her go in first. She crossed the room and stood in front of his desk.

Joyce had worked for him since he was named chief of staff for Senator Lawson. Six years. She knew him well, and that meant catching him when she could. She was a master at timing his entrances and exits. She was smart, discreet and damned good at her job, Claude thought. What he appreciated most was that she never wielded her sexuality. Joyce Holden was stunning. She was an exotic mix of East Indian and African American with a luminous honey-brown complexion, wide dark eyes and silky black hair that hung like a veil to the middle of her back. Her body rivaled a Victoria's Secret model. He'd been hesitant about hiring her for all of those reasons. He didn't need or want the distraction. But her professional demeanor dwarfed her allure. He gave her a chance and there wasn't a day that he'd regretted his decision. They were co-workers, equals and friends. He wouldn't be able to manage without her.

He took off his jacket. His stark white shirt appeared to gleam against his rich chocolate complexion. There was a line of women in D.C. who vied for Claude's attention, Joyce thought. She placed the folder on his desk and opened it. What she admired about him was that he never mixed business with pleasure. In all the years she'd worked for him, there was never even a whisper of impropriety. He was often the topic of discussion among the female staffers. They all wanted her take on his availability and their chances with him. Her answer was always the same: "Set your sights elsewhere." She was one of the few people that knew anything about his personal life and what had scarred him. Her loyalty and admiration of him would never allow her to share that knowledge.

"These are the staff reviews that you approved for this quarter." She lifted them out of the folder and handed them to him one at a time.

As chief of staff he was responsible for more than one hundred employees who were part of Senator Lawson's team, from file clerks to committee members. It was his job to know each and every one of them by name, their responsibilities and their ability to do what they were hired to do. He also took time to get to know them personally, their families, their long-term ambitions, their shortcomings and strengths. If the team looked good, Senator Lawson looked good. He had the senator's ear and his complete confidence, and every member of the team knew that if they wanted to get ahead they needed to stay on the right side of Claude Montgomery.

"Long weekend coming up," he said, glancing at the document in front of him. "Any special plans?" He scrawled his signature at the bottom. Joyce handed him the next file.

"Me and Luke and the kids are going to Seattle to spend some time with his parents."

"How is his mother?"

She handed him another document. "Better. But she hasn't been the same since the stroke."

He glanced up and caught the unhappy look in her eyes. "I'm sorry. I wish there was something else I could do. I know it must be a real strain on Luke."

"You've done more than anyone could ask. The therapist and home attendant that you got for her has made a world of difference and took a lot of weight off of Luke's and his father's shoulders. We can't thank you enough."

He waved off the sentiment. "If you need more time, just let me know. We'll work it out."

They pushed through the paperwork and finally closed the folder.

"Your flight leaves in an hour. I have the car waiting for you outside."

He stood and grabbed his jacket from the back of his chair. She walked to the corner and handed him his briefcase on his way out of the door.

They walked out together.

"Try to enjoy yourself. I know how much you hate those gatherings."

He groaned. "I'll try."

"Have a safe trip," she said.

He walked out of the building and into the late afternoon breeze. "Thanks." He waved goodbye and jogged down the stairs to the waiting Lincoln Town Car.

Within moments he was reclining against the lush interior upholstery of the car and speeding through the streets of D.C. Before long the iconic images of the White House, the Washington Monument and the Capitol building became smaller until they disappeared in the distance.

He leaned back against the soft leather and closed his eyes. Getting out of town and back to his home in Westchester was always something that he looked forward to. It was an opportunity for him to unwind and shed the rigors and stress that confronted him in his life in Washington. Unfortunately, the demands of the job didn't allow him to get home as often as he would have liked. That reality pricked him more so today. Rather than roaming the cozy rooms of his home, listening to music, maybe catching up with a friend or taking his bike out for a spin along New York's highways, he was going home to get ready for a stuffy black-tie dinner. The very thing he worked at not doing—at least as much as he could.

He had Alan Harte to thank for this one, he thought, as he followed the line of boarding passengers and took his seat in coach. Alan could convince the devil to change his ways. He smiled to himself.

They'd been friends for years from Claude's early days of doing community work back in his home state of Louisiana. Alan was newly divorced and climbing up the ranks at the State Department. They'd met during an education forum in Baton Rouge and had been friends ever since. It was Alan who'd introduced him to Senator Lawson.

They tried to get together as often as they could, but with Alan's constant traveling and Claude's busy schedule it was often difficult. So when Alan strong-armed him into attending an embassy event, he relented for old times' sake. He'd said that it was high time that Claude had a woman in his life—not that Alan ever would again—and that his sister Melanie was the one who could make magic happen.

Claude had no real interest in a permanent relationship. At least he didn't think he did. But in the weeks leading up to today the notion began to take shape in his head. When he looked at his life, it was a complete success. He had what most longed for. Yet, there were times when the loneliness of his life hit him. Like today, when Joyce talked about her husband and kids and visiting relatives during the brief time off. Most days he didn't miss that kind of thing. But more often than he cared to admit he'd begun to long for a life that he'd almost had—once.

He fastened his seatbelt and opened his copy of *The Washington Post.* He turned to the arts and entertainment section.

The captain announced that they were next in line for takeoff and they should be landing at New York's LaGuardia airport on time.

He folded the newspaper on his lap, leaned back and shut his eyes. Might as well catch a quick nap, he thought. He had a long night ahead of him. As he drifted off into a light sleep he wondered fleetingly if Alan's sister was as good as he claimed she was. He'd always spoken of her in such glowing terms, and curiously enough in the years that he and Alan had been friends, Claude had never met Melanie.

He'd seen pictures and he'd often wondered if she was as attractive in person. There was something about her smile and her eyes that drew him. And he often wondered with the business that she was in if there was a man in her life. He'd never ask Alan anything like that, so it was ironic that their first meeting would be with her in the role of matchmaker for him.

He was the last person to even think about using a dating service, but Alan insisted it was much more than that—and he'd guarantee a wonderful outcome.

"Then why don't you use it?" Claude had asked after Alan had all but browbeaten him into attending the gala and meeting Melanie.

"First of all, I'm family. That would be like winning the sweepstakes grand prize and being an employee of the company that sponsored it."

Claude just looked at him, shook his head and chuckled. "Whatever, man. I'm only doing this because we're friends."

Alan slapped him on the back. "You won't regret it. Promise."

That remained to be seen, Claude thought as he finally put his key in the door to his Westchester home. It remained to be seen.

Chapter 2

Melanie had been to her share of high-class soirees—from Paris to the Caribbean, rubbing elbows with athletes, billionaires, movie and television stars, corporate moguls and media-shy executives. But it was always a treat to be in the company of real power, the political machine that made the decisions about everything from health care to appointments to the Supreme Court. There was an unmistakable energy that emanated from the men and women in politics that could be found nowhere else in the world. For Melanie, it was a definite turn on.

Tonight the party was being hosted by the newly named American ambassador to Spain, which decidedly influenced the evening's décor, entertainment and menu.

Alan escorted his small entourage through security and took them into the grand ballroom. When Alan said black tie, he wasn't kidding. The men were decked out in tuxedos, some with tails and cummerbunds. The women perfectly complemented their escorts' attire in cocktail dresses and evening gowns. But it was the jewelry that competed for attention, sparkling from ears, wrists and throats with enough joint wattage to light up the heavens.

Melanie preferred cocktail dresses over full-length gowns. She had great legs and used every opportunity to show them off. Tonight she'd chosen a bronze Vera Wang dress that was so close to her natural skin tone that she almost appeared naked were it not for the rhinestone appliqué that framed her décolletage. Her stilettos, in a matching color, accentuated her five-foot-nine height. The dress hugged her upper body, dipped dangerously low in the back and flared from the waist to just above her knees.

A trio of Spanish guitarists played in the background as the wait staff, outfitted in traditional dress, moved in and around the well-heeled crowd.

"You probably know a lot of these people," Alan said as he and Melanie made their way across the room, nodding and smiling at familiar faces.

Vincent had taken his wife, sister and cousin to get drinks while Alan and Melanie mingled.

Alan lifted his chin. "There's Claude over by the balcony talking to the attorney general."

Melanie followed the direction of Alan's gaze and spotted Claude. Perhaps it was the timing, a sixth sense or kismet, but he turned his head in her direction at the very moment she focused on him.

A sudden rush like that feeling you get in the pit of your stomach when the roller coaster drops down from its highest point at breakneck speed swept through her. Air shot up from her lungs and lodged in the center of her chest. His eyes, as dark and mysterious as the edge of the universe, held her in place. The barest hint of a smile teased his mouth and her before he gave her an imperceptible nod and turned back to his conversation.

Claude Montgomery was a standout in any room. There was a commanding air about him, a swagger that amplified his deep chocolate skin, broad chest and long legs. Wearing an Armani tux, Claude Montgomery was damn-near edible. He was a shoe-in for Idris Elba's better-looking brother. Whoever was lucky enough to land him was in for a treat—at least in the looks department. She'd have a better idea once they did his profile. In the meantime she needed to regain her composure and quit imagining herself naked in his bed.

"Come on. I'll introduce you," Alan said, oblivious to the shift in her world that had just taken place.

The last time Melanie was nervous about meeting a man was in fifth grade when she got called into Principal Harrison's office for starting a hunger strike in the lunchroom to protest the lousy food. That was a long time ago. But she hadn't forgotten the racing pulse, wobbly knees and damp palms.

As they approached, the conversation drew to an end when the attorney general was pulled away by his wife.

Claude deposited his empty glass on the tray of a passing waiter. His broad smile was in full effect as he extended his hand to Alan.

"Good to see you, Al," he said, shaking his hand heartily while slapping him on the back with the other.

They both turned to Melanie and there was that look again that seemed to suck her into his soul.

"Claude, this is my sister Melanie. Mel, Claude Montgomery."

The seas parted and disappeared into the background. It was only the two of them waiting to cross that great divide.

Melanie reacted first. "Alan has been singing your praises," she said, extending her hand toward him.

Claude took her slender fingers in his hand and brought them to his lips. He placed a feather-like kiss on the back of her hand. "Your reputation precedes you," he said, his voice low and throbbing like distant thunder.

"I do hope that's a good thing," she said forcing herself not to concentrate on the currents of electricity that shot up and down her arm.

"Most definitely. Can I get you a drink?"

"Thank you. Yes."

He raised his hand and signaled for a waiter, who was at their side almost instantly. He plucked a glass of champagne from the tray and handed it to her.

"Thank you." She took a tiny sip. "Alan says you're chief of staff for Senator Lawson. I'm surprised we haven't met before."

"I try to stay away from these shindigs whenever possible," he said with a gleam in his eyes.

Melanie grinned.

"I'll let you two get acquainted. I'm going to look for my son and company," Alan pressed Melanie's shoulder and walked off.

"So, Alan tells me that you are the consummate matchmaker."

Melanie lowered her gaze for a moment. "That's the rumor," she answered, her tone teasing. "And I understand that you may be interested in our services."

Claude drew in a long breath. "I've been consider-ing it for a while now," he said, the levity gone from his voice. "My job takes up a great deal of my time and I believe I'm reaching the point where I'd like to come home to more than paperwork, my BlackBerry and cognac."

Hmm, he likes cognac. A man with taste.

"I see. Believe me, I totally understand. If I didn't know better I'd think I was talking to my brother."

Claude chuckled. "I don't think Alan will ever settle down again. He lives and breathes his job."

"Tell me, what type of woman are you looking for?"

His deep gaze played across her face, like the sun warming the earth, and something stirred inside of her.

"There you are."

They turned in unison to see Senator Lawson come up beside them.

"Melanie. Melanie Harte?"

Melanie beamed. "How are you Bradford?"

He captured her in a hug. "I had no idea you'd be here. What a pleasant surprise."

"It's good to see you, too."

"I knew her grandmother, God rest her sweet soul. I watched this little lady grow up. Her grandmother introduced me to my late wife Louisa and the rest is history," he ended with a wistful chuckle. He lowered his voice. "I understand you took over the business."

Melanie nodded. "I did, along with my nieces and nephew."

"Wonderful! We'll have to talk before the night is over. I want you to meet my son Rafe." He looked around. "If you'll excuse me, I want to catch Senator Morgan before he tries to slip out." He lightly bussed Melanie's cheek. "Don't leave before we talk."

"I won't," she promised, squeezing his hand.

The newest Supreme Court justice walked by and waved at Melanie.

"Congratulations," Melanie mouthed.

"Call me," she said in return before being swept into a crowd of senators vying for her attention.

"You travel in lofty circles," Claude said, finishing off his drink.

"My grandmother and then my mother traveled in these circles all their lives. They made sure that I knew everyone that they did. I really don't think about it much. It's part of my life, which happens to help with the business that I'm in. I'm totally unimpressed by status and celebrity at this point. Once you strip that all away, the real person emerges. That's who I want to get to know. And most of them, once you get beyond their public personas, they're just regular folks with the same wants, needs, flaws and fears as everyone else. They simply have the money and the power to hide it better than the rest."

"Point taken." He paused a moment. "So what do you see beneath my layer?"

She looked up into his eyes. Her heart suddenly thumped. "That's what we'll have to find out. Won't we?"

"You've been monopolizing this beautiful woman all night, Claude."

Claude turned to his left. "Rafe. Your father was just looking for you."

Rafe chuckled and his light-brown eyes sparkled in the light. "I'm sure he was," he murmured, the hint of his Louisiana accent seeping through. He stepped closer and zeroed in on Melanie. "Raford Lawson," he said, taking her hand.

"Melanie Harte."

"My pleasure." He kissed her hand. "Dance with me."

She hesitated a moment. "Of course. Please excuse me, Claude."

Claude gave a short nod of his head as Rafe escorted Melanie onto the dance floor.

"So Melanie Harte, what brings you to this stuffy affair?" He took her hand in his—the other went to the small of her back as they swayed to the music.

Melanie laughed lightly. "My brother Alan invited me."

He arched his neck back and looked down into her face. "Alan Harte is your brother?"

"Yes, he is."

"Well I'll be damned," he said over his laughter. "You're *that* Melanie Harte. Your grandmother fixed up my daddy and mama."

"So the story goes."

He stepped back, released her and made a gallant bow. "I am in the arms of greatness," he teased.

Melanie shook her head and chuckled. "You are much too dramatic."

He swept her back into his arms and whispered deep in her ear. "I've been called much worse."

They danced together for two more songs before Melanie begged off.

"Save the last dance for me," Rafe said with a light kiss on her cheek.

He was definitely a charmer, she thought with amusement as she watched him saunter away toward a group of beautiful women, who all but swooned when he approached. Melanie shook her head and smiled.

"I see you've already become acquainted with my son," Senator Lawson said.

Melanie turned in his direction. "Yes. He's certainly a charmer."

The senator chuckled. "Oh, is that what you call it?"

"What would you call it?"

"Oh, I'd never say what I thought to a lady." He

winked. "But I will say that he needs taming. Rafe is a free spirit. Can't get him to settle down to anything serious. But I think the right woman could do what me and the whole damn family have not been able to," he said, his Creole background filtering through. "That's where you come in. I'd like to secure your services."

"Are you sure he would be agreeable?"

"Every now and again I can get the boy to listen to me. And if it has anything to do with women, he'll listen."

Melanie's right brow rose for an instant. "I'm sure we could find someone special for your son."

"Good. I'm counting on it. I want Rafe to step into my shoes one day and I want him to have a good woman at his side—someone strong enough to stand up against some of his foolishness."

She drew in a breath, reached in her purse and handed him her card. "If he's willing and when he's ready, have him call me."

The senator took the card and tucked it into his jacket pocket. "It will be sooner than you think."

Melanie moved around the room, chatting with many of the familiar faces and catching up on the political gossip. Throughout the evening she caught glimpses of Claude and each time her insides quaked. It was clear that he was a man completely comfortable in who he was and how he'd gotten there. She noticed the way he held his muscular body, never lording his height over people but rather inviting them into his space. He focused on people when they talked as if they were the only person in the world that mattered. He was intelligent, witty, a great dancer and well-connected. Yes, on the surface, Claude Montgomery was a man that any woman would desire. Not to mention that his sex appeal was off the charts.

Then there was Raford Lawson. There was no doubt that Rafe could charm a blind woman out of her panties. He was breathtakingly gorgeous from the natural waves of his ink black hair, the honey brown of his eyes, his dark sweeping brows down to his imported Italian shoes. He was wealthy, spoiled and brought up to believe that he could have whatever he wanted. He was like an unbridled Arabian stallion: magnificent and wild, never harnessed and never ridden. His father was right. It would take a special woman to rein in Rafe Lawson. Inwardly, she smiled. The Platinum Society would certainly have their work cut out for them.

As the family was preparing to leave, Raford stopped Melanie at the door. He took a sip of his bourbon. "My father insists that you can find me the perfect woman." He extracted the card his father had given him from his pocket and held it between his two fingers.

"It's what we do." A glint lit her eyes.

The corner of his exquisite mouth curved upward. "You're on Ms. Harte. Expect my call." He winked and walked away.

"What was that about?" Veronica asked, draping her wrap across her shoulders.

Melanie turned to her niece. "It seems that we may have two new clients instead of one."

"What do you think about Claude?" Alan asked as they headed back to Sag Harbor, cocooned in the luxury of a stretch limousine. Everyone chimed in except Melanie. Sensing she was being scrutinized, she glanced up and focused.

"What?"

"You were definitely someplace else," Alan teased. "I was asking what you thought of Claude."

That's exactly who she was thinking of when she'd zoned out of the conversation. "I'm sure we can find someone for him. On the surface he totally fits our criteria. Of course we'll know much better after Veronica works up his profile."

"And Senator Lawson wants us to find someone for his son," Veronica added.

"Rafe?" Alan asked, clearly surprised.

Melanie nodded her head. "That's what he told me."

"And Rafe agreed?"

"He told me in no uncertain terms that I would

be hearing from him," Melanie said. "It was almost a challenge."

Alan chuckled and leaned back against the plush leather seats. "Trust me, it will be."

"Rafe, are you ready to leave? I'm tired."

Rafe turned his gaze away from the entourage as they said their good-nights. He focused on the lovely woman in front of him. For a moment he couldn't recall her name. It didn't matter really. They all loved being called sweetheart or baby. He set down his glass on the tray of a passing waiter and turned his hundred-watt smile on his date.

"Not too tired," he teased, trailing his finger along the curve of her exposed back.

She purred with pleasure and moved closer to him. "Never too tired for you. You should know that by now."

He probably should, he thought while he absently nuzzled her neck, imagining Melanie's warm caramel skin beneath his lips. The truth was this woman who was ready to do whatever he asked was one of so many like her. Beautiful, nameless women that saw the Lawson name, heard whispers about his skills in the bedroom and put themselves in his path. He loved women. All types of women. Tall, thin, thick, short, black, white, Latina, Asian. They were all wonderful, willing and desirable in their own way.

And the southern gentleman in him compelled him to please as many of them as he could.

His trio of sisters—Lee Ann and the twins Dominique and Desiree—steered all of their friends clear of their playboy brother and admonished the youngest Lawson, their brother Justin, not to follow in their big brother's footsteps.

Rafe grinned to himself as he helped his date with her wrap. He loved his family dearly, even though he constantly remained on the receiving end of their reprimands. But no amount of scolding, threats of being cut out of the family fortune or hints of scandal stopped him in his relentless pursuit of women.

It was in his nature. It was in his blood as sure as the champagne that flowed through it now. He accepted that. He knew that deep inside he was looking for something. He simply didn't know what that something was and he would not stop until he found it.

Rafe slid into the back seat of the chauffeured limo. He tossed his tuxedo jacket across to the other side of the horseshoe-shaped leather seat. He leaned toward the mini bar and uncorked a bottle of wine. He poured a glass for himself and his date, confident that before the night was over her name would come back to him.

"Rafe," she cooed, leaning forward to expose her

heavenly depths. "I was hoping you'd like to join me and some close friends for a weekend in Cancun."

He looked at her over the rim of the flute. Her makeup was a little too heavy and he concluded it was to mask her acne. Her body was lovely but he could tell from experience that it didn't come naturally. She did have interesting eyes and a lovely mouth. Kissable. That much he did remember.

"Sounds appealing."

"Say yes." She all but batted her eyelashes.

It was as if the action lifted the veil that had covered his eyes and he wondered why he was with her. What was he doing? "I'll check my schedule and get back to you." He smiled to soften the disappointment. "Where do you live again, cher? Forgive me." He held up his glass. "One too many."

"Park and 62nd Street."

"Of course." He winked at her and tapped on the partition that separated them from the driver.

The Plexiglas whirred downward.

"Park and 62nd," Rafe instructed. He reclined against the thick leather back seat. He ignored her pout.

"I thought we were going to your place," she whined.

"I'm sorry, cher. Not tonight. Maybe another time."

She flopped back against the seat and folded her

arms tightly to her body, elevating the expensive enhancements. Rafe turned his attention to the traffic outside the window, lighting up the night sky with the gleam from streetlights that danced off their hoods, their headlights illuminating onto the blacktop. It seemed to create a magical lightshow, much like his life. It was all smoke and mirrors. He'd mastered the art of illusion. The ability to charm and woo, to talk his way into and out of anything he wanted.

He draped his arm along the back of the seat and drummed his long fingers against the firm surface. He hated these introspective moments, those times when all of the scolding, threats and warnings from his family stirred his conscience. In those moments he came face to face with the pointlessness of the life that he led.

His father was a powerful senator, his sister Lee Ann had the education, skills and family lineage to move into politics. The twins, when they weren't trying to spend the family fortune, were both involved in philanthropy. His brother Justin was being primed for the political arena. Rafe's unambitious lifestyle went against everything that the Lawson family stood for.

"Much as I loved your mother, God rest her soul, she spoiled you rotten, boy. Doted on you like you were the king of damned England and enabled all of your philandering ways," Bradford Lawson had said, glaring at his son with the same vehemence that he reserved for his opponents on the senate floor.

Rafe endured the periodic tongue-lashing from his father with practiced chagrin. There was probably some truth to what his father said, although he would never admit it to him. His beloved mother had been his rock, the only one in the family who understood him. She knew how to rein him in without holding him in place.

God he missed her. There was an emptiness in his soul since she'd been gone and he filled it with one woman after another, wild parties, good liquor and tabloid-worthy adventures. For a while the space would be filled, but inevitably the emptiness would return.

Maybe his father was right. Maybe he did need a good woman in his life to help him settle down. And his thoughts shifted to Melanie.

She was different from the other women he had known and bedded. She couldn't care less who he was. She was independent and didn't appear to need the arm of a man to make herself look good or feel important. She already was—all qualities that were rare in the women he saw. *Melanie Harte.*

"You're smiling again," his date said, cutting into his thoughts. He turned from the window and realized that she was sitting right by his side. "I thought I'd done something to upset you."

His smile wavered and held. He stretched a finger toward her chin and gently lifted it. Yes, she had beautiful eyes and kissable lips. He remembered now. Her name was Stephanie. His gaze caressed her slightly over-made-up face. He leaned forward and pressed his lips toward her kissable ones. She sighed ever so softly.

"Should we bring the wine up to your place?" he said against her mouth. He felt her body loosen with delighted relief.

The idea that he was the source of her happiness, real or imagined, only helped to reaffirm his mantra. He couldn't disappoint a woman. After all, he was a southern gentleman.

The car pulled to a stop in front of Stephanie's building on Park Avenue. The driver opened the door. Rafe stepped out first and helped Stephanie to her feet. He slipped his arm around her waist and pulled her close to his side.

She laughed and it was the music that always made him weak, made him dance—the sound of a woman's laughter.

He walked behind her as the building doorman greeted her. She turned, her smile bright and her eyes inviting.

His dimple appeared. The elevator door closed behind them. He'd let Melanie Harte try to reform him tomorrow.

Chapter 3

When Melanie walked into her office the following day, the team had already assembled. No matter how appealing a client might be or how much money they had, it was protocol that the decision to take on a new client was unanimous.

"Hey, Aunt Mel," the trio said in unison.

"Morning, troops." She set her cup of coffee on the side table. "Everyone have a good time last night?"

"Absolutely," they agreed.

Melanie took a sip of her coffee and settled down on the overstuffed couch. Her office was an eclectic blend of functionality and comfort. Her high-tech equipment was housed inside floor-to-ceiling wooden cabinets that were rolled out for use. The video screen was mounted on the wall for full presentations of clients and their prospects. The bay windows looked out onto the bluffs and ocean beyond. Pale peach walls were adorned with one-of-a-kind pieces of art. Glass and chrome were the focal accessories, with conversational seating throughout. Fresh flowers graced the tables, shipped in weekly from the florist. This was TPS central, where all of the decisions were made.

"I've done some preliminary work on Mr. Montgomery and Mr. Lawson," Veronica said, "based on observation and what I was able to pull from the Internet. I'll have a full profile of each once we set up the meeting."

"You certainly didn't waste any time," Melanie said. "Let's see what you have so far."

Veronica pressed a button on the console and the screen lit up. The first screen was filled with basic data about Claude and Rafe—date of birth, physicality, where they lived, profession, education and relationship status.

Melanie stared at the near life-sized images of Claude and felt her body come alive in response. She knew she'd have to keep her lusty thoughts to herself if she was going to be effective in finding a suitable match for him.

The sound of male voices coming in their direction

drew everyone's attention. Moments later Alan stuck his head in the door.

"I thought I smelled smoke," Alan joked. "All this brain power brushing up against each other like kindling."

"Very funny," Melanie said.

"I brought company."

Claude stepped into the frame of the door. "Good morning."

"Morning."

Melanie's heart banged in her chest and a sudden rush of heat flooded her body. She shifted in her seat, reached for her coffee cup, realized her hands were shaking and changed her mind. She folded her hands in her lap.

"He insisted that I stop by today," Claude explained. "I told him I should have called first for an appointment." He was talking to everyone in the room, but his gaze had settled on Melanie.

Her throat was bone dry.

"Not a problem," Jessica said. "Roni was just going over your preliminaries."

"Was she?" Claude's brows rose in question. "And what might those be?"

"Basic data," Veronica said matter of factly. In addition to being the profiler of the business, Veronica was an Internet and computer whiz. If there was a grain of sand to be found, Veronica would find it. She had search programs and software that Melanie didn't want to know anything about. Google was archaic as far as Veronica was concerned.

"It's all protocol," Melanie said, finally finding her voice. "We build a profile on all of our clients. It's how we make an appropriate match."

Claude crossed the room. Melanie caught a subtle whiff of his scent. Her pulse fluttered. He sat down in one of the matching side chairs.

"Sounds very…calculated, for lack of a better word."

"Part calculation, part chemistry," Jessica offered. "Our responsibility is to match the wants and desires, intelligence and personality of two people, and ask all the questions that two people who are attracted to each other never ask until it's too late."

Claude stretched his long legs out in front of him. Alan clapped him heartily on the shoulder. "They're really pretty harmless," he teased.

Claude glanced up at his friend. "You sure? I sorta feel like a science project."

"Once we match you up with the woman of your dreams, you'll forget all about this technical stuff," Melanie said with a wave of her hand.

Claude zeroed in on Melanie. "Is that a promise?" His eyes moved across her face, heating everywhere they landed.

Melanie slowly stood. "You're in very good

hands." She picked up her mug and walked out. Alan followed.

"Thanks for doing this, sis."

"Sure. Business is business. Claude seems like a good guy. I'm sure we'll find someone for him."

Melanie caught the serious tone in his voice. She looked across at her brother. "What aren't you telling me?"

"Nothing that you won't find out."

Melanie stopped walking and folded her arms. "If there's something I need to know, tell me, Alan."

Alan inhaled deeply. He dug his hands into his pants pockets. "About ten years ago, Claude was engaged. On his wedding day, his fiancé's limo was in an accident on her way to the church." He looked down.

Melanie's hand went to her chest. "Oh, I…I'm sorry." Her eyes flew toward her office. She could see Claude in conversation with the team, fully engaged, laughing and nodding. Her spirit ached. She knew all too well about that kind of loss, the emptiness that was left behind. After Steven she had her grandmother and her mother to pull her through and then the business. Who had been there for Claude? Had he ever found closure? Was his job all he had? The questions nagged at her like an itch in the center of your back—difficult to get to.

"He's not like me. He's more than his job," Alan

said as if reading her thoughts. He leaned down and kissed her cheek. "I'm going to run into town. Buzz me on my cell when your team has finished picking my man apart." He winked and strode out, leaving Melanie with thoughts of Claude swirling in her head.

Melanie was in her sitting room, putting together the list of potential guests for her annual Summer Jam. Claude left several hours earlier with Alan and was given the assurance that TPS would be in touch with him shortly. Vincent logged in Claude's $25,000 deposit and created a file for him. Jessica and Veronica were busy putting together a complete profile of Claude based on their extensive interview.

As hard as she tried, she couldn't keep her mind on the task at hand. Her thoughts and unsettled emotions kept getting in the way. Giving into her frustration, she closed the social calendar software program on her computer with the intention of getting a light snack. Just as she got up, her office phone rang. It was nearly five o'clock, the official end of the business day, she thought, mildly annoyed. She started to let it go to voicemail when she thought about the mantra of her business. "It's never too late or too early to deal with a paying or potential client."

"The Platinum Society, Melanie Harte speaking," she answered in her cheerful professional voice.

"I would think you would have someone else

doing the mundane task of answering the phone," the definitively male voice said, the slight Creole accent unmistakably that of Rafe Lawson. "However, I couldn't be happier that it's you."

"Mr. Lawson." She sat back down.

He chuckled. "Ah, the lady remembers."

"I tend not to forget names, faces and voices."

"I'll keep that in mind."

"What can I do for you?"

"I'm picking up where we left off. My father is insistent that I find myself a suitable woman who can make an honest man out of me. You indicated that you were up for the challenge."

"My company," she clarified, not wanting to head off in the wrong direction.

"Of course." He breathed into the phone. "So… where do we begin?"

"I'll switch you over to Jessica, and she'll set up an appointment."

"I'm leaving for the West Coast tomorrow afternoon. I hope you can slip me in before then."

His statement sounded innocent enough, but Melanie didn't miss the sexual innuendo. She chose to ignore it.

"If there is a time slot, I'm sure we will accommodate you."

"Actually it would only take a little over an hour to drive out there. You're in Sag Harbor?"

"You've done your homework."

"I like to know who I'm getting in bed with…so to speak."

Melanie's body flushed. "Hold on a moment." She placed the call on hold and pressed the button for the main office. Veronica picked up.

"Hey Aunt Mel, what's up?"

"I have Raford Lawson on the line. He wants an appointment as soon as possible. He's leaving to go out of town tomorrow afternoon."

"Let me check with Jess."

Melanie tapped her manicured nails against the table while she waited.

"We can see him this evening if he's really insistent or first thing tomorrow at nine."

"Thanks. I'll get right back to you."

She took Raford off hold. "Tonight at seven or tomorrow morning at nine. Your choice."

"The sooner the better. I'll see you shortly." He hung up without saying goodbye, a testament to his arrogance.

Slowly Melanie hung up the receiver. Her gut told her that Raford Lawson was going to be a handful of trouble. And she was just the one to put him in his place, even if he was a senator's son.

Chapter 4

Melanie called an impromptu meeting with the team after she got off the phone with Raford. They all sat around the conference table and waited for Melanie to bring them up to speed.

"As you all know, Raford Lawson will be here this evening. From the brief conversations I've had with him, he'll be a challenge for lack of a better word. And not because he is unmatchable, but because he seems to believe that this is all a game and he's doing this to appease his father."

"We can say no based on his interview," Veronica said.

"I don't think Senator Lawson is someone we want

to offend. After all, Grandma Harte found him his wife."

They all hummed in agreement.

"How bad can he be?" Jessica asked.

Melanie didn't want to let on that Rafe had all but tried to openly seduce her. She could handle him without involving them. And she didn't want her assessment to interfere with their evaluation.

"Let's just say that his reputation as a consummate flirt and certified playboy may very well be warranted. However, that won't keep us from doing the best job possible for our paying clients. Besides, I'd love to be able to say TPS made the match for playboy Lawson." She folded her arms and grinned.

"From the little I've turned up on him so far, his string of broken hearts is long and illustrious," Veronica said. "He's been tied to damn near everyone but the Queen of England."

They all shared a laugh.

"Busy man," Vincent said absently, returning his attention to his computer screen, which detailed the current expenditures and income. "We're really in solid shape," he added. "If Mr. Lawson did become the 'exception,' his loss wouldn't cause a blip on my screen." He tapped the screen with his index finger and glanced at all of them with a self-satisfied smile. "Besides, the investments that I've made on our behalf throughout the years have made each of us contemptuously wealthy. We only took a minor hit with the economic meltdown. We're in good shape."

Melanie winked at her nephew. She turned her attention to Veronica. "We'll want to get both of the profiles done as soon as possible. Unfortunately for us, both of our clients have very erratic schedules."

"I understand. It's my top priority. I've entered all of Mr. Montgomery's info into the databank. Then I'll flip it to the personality software program. I should have a pretty good picture rather soon."

"Great." Melanie pushed up from her seat and stood. "I'm going to get back to my party list. Let me know when Mr. Lawson arrives." She returned to her office and attempted to get back to where she'd left off. Her annual holiday party was the event of the season at the Harbor. Everyone who was anyone was in attendance. It was always a spectacular affair and plenty of fun, but it was quite the task to put it all together.

She continued compiling her list from her electronic address book, and her thoughts continued to drift to Claude. Her fingers slowed then stopped as she found herself staring out the window, watching the late-day waves crash against the shore. It was serene and turbulent all at once. The overhanging muted orange of the impending evening created a feeling of solitude, an aloneness within her. And

Melanie realized with a start that it was what she was feeling inside, and meeting Claude had stirred the lonely beast within her.

Melanie shook her head, dispelling the images and the marauding thoughts. Since when had she become so reflective? She laughed lightly and crossed the room to the small cabinet built into the wall. She opened the wood door and took out a bottle of white wine and a glass. Returning to the window she sat down on the cushioned bench, tucked herself into the corner and sipped her wine. She leaned back against the embracing frame and momentarily closed her eyes, savoring the flavor of the wine.

One day she would turn the business over to the family, she mused, the way it had been done for generations. She'd be much older, hopefully wiser and comfortably wealthy and she wondered if she'd wind up spending her sunset years alone.

A light knock on her door scattered her thoughts. "Yes, come in."

Jessica stuck her head in the door. "Mr. Lawson just arrived," she said, her eyes sparkling and a commercial perfect smile flashing. "He's gorgeous," she gushed. "His pictures do him no justice."

Melanie smiled benignly. If nothing else could be said about Rafe Lawson it was that he was worth the time spent looking at him.

Melanie put her glass down but didn't get up. "Very good. Get him settled and get started. Let me know when he's ready to leave.'

Jessica's eyes widened. "Aren't you going to come and say hello?"

Melanie pressed her lips together before speaking. "Ill be sure to see him before he leaves."

Jessica frowned for a moment but knew better than to push her aunt. She shrugged her left shoulder and backed out of the door.

Melanie exhaled slowly. She knew from her first meeting with Raford Lawson that it would be best for all concerned if she limited her contact with him. However, Rafe was used to getting what he wanted and moments later he made his wants clear. Veronica was at the door.

"Yes, come in."

"Aunt Mel," she began as a tight line of annoyance tugged her brows closer together. "Mr. Lawson insists on only dealing with you." She planted her hands on her hips.

"Did you tell him I was busy?"

"Of course. And I told him that you don't deal with preparing the profile—I do. He acted like I'd told him the biggest joke."

Melanie bit back a smile. She knew how seriously her family took their jobs and Veronica in particular.

Melanie switched off her computer. "I'll be right out. Have him wait for me in the small conference room and ask Evan to bring us some refreshments, please."

Veronica huffed and did as she was asked.

Melanie opened her desk drawer, took out her compact and dabbed away the shine from her nose, added a splash of lipstick, then went out to join Mr. Lawson.

When she walked across the wide foyer to the intimate office space that only comfortably sat four, she found Raford with his back to her perusing the artwork on the muted candy-apple-red walls.

He turned at the sound of her heels on the inlaid wood floors. His smile was slow and devastating, darkening his molasses-colored eyes even as they lit up the room and zeroed in on her.

This was the casual playboy in front of her—not the distinguished gentleman from the embassy. Gone was the formal tuxedo, replaced today with a chocolate-colored cotton-knit sweater over a pair of jeans and Italian loafers the color of his sweater. A platinum watch peeked out from the cuff of his sleeve and a tiny diamond stud sparkled in his ear. The heady, manly scent of his very expensive cologne drew her into the room and wrapped around her in a welcoming embrace.

Melanie swallowed over the dry knot in her

throat, then boldly strode forward, hand extended. "Mr. Lawson, I understand you're giving my team a hard time," she said, the hint of a reprimanding smile teasing her mouth.

He grinned as he took her hand. "First, my daddy is Mr. Lawson, or Senator as he often prefers to be called—even by his children," he added, his eyes twinkling with mischief. He brushed his thumb seductively across her knuckles, sending a shiver up her arm. He brought her hand to his lips and placed a feathery light kiss on it, his eyes never leaving hers. When he lifted his head, he said to her, "Everyone calls me Rafe, even my enemies," he added with a chuckle.

Melanie eased her hand from his grasp. "I can't imagine you having enemies, not with all that charm you ooze."

Rafe tossed his head back and laughed full out, a deep and warm sound. "I see we're going to get along just fine."

"I'm sure we will," she said as Evan quietly placed a tray of fruit, crackers and imported cheeses on the table and exited as stealthily as he'd entered. "Our goal at The Platinum Society is to treat every client as if they were the only one. Which is why I can assure you that you won't have any problems and will get the best attention from my team. They are all experts at what they do."

Rafe picked a slice of pineapple off the tray and popped it into his mouth, chewing softly. "I was hoping that you and I would be going over the details."

"I'm afraid not. Once the assessment is done, I'll review it with the team and make my recommendations. At that point, you and I will meet again."

The corner of his mouth curved upward. "Well, if talking to your team will quicken you and me talking again, then let's get started."

Melanie's stomach knotted for a moment. "Rafe, we need to be clear. I don't mix up my business with my personal life and I don't see clients outside of the office."

Rafe stepped up to her, clouding her brain with his scent. "Cher, don't take yourself so seriously. I would never want you to compromise your ethics. Is that what you thought?" His brow arched. His sarcastic question hung in the air, taunting her.

She ran her tongue lightly across her dry lips. "The team is waiting."

"Lead the way."

Melanie turned to head out and could feel him cataloging every inch of her. For good measure she put a little more sway in her hips. Let him get a good look at what he'd never have.

* * *

Jessica and Veronica were waiting for them in the main office.

Rafe turned to Melanie at the door. "Will I see you before I leave?"

The tone of his question, soft, almost tender, stroked her center like a single finger trailing across her skin.

"If I'm done with my own work, I'll be sure to say goodbye. In the meantime, try to behave yourself." Before he could respond, she walked away, closing the door gently behind her.

Melanie returned to her private office and sealed herself away, determined to get her list in order. But the exercise was initially futile. Images of Claude then Rafe danced through her head. What she needed was a man of her own so that she could stop salivating over men she would have to turn over to other women.

More than two hours later, Melanie had finally made some serious headway with her list and moved on to sketching out the menu, theme and entertainment. Humming to herself, her brief moment of self-satisfaction was interrupted by Jessica at the door. Melanie turned away from her computer and realized that evening had fully descended upon the island. In the distance from her window she could see the yellow dots of lights begin to fill the windows of the homes on the bluff. She stretched. "Come on in Jess," she said over a muffled yawn.

Jessica stepped partially in. "We're done. Mr. Lawson wanted to say good-night."

I bet he does, Melanie thought. She got up, adjusted her top and followed Jessica out. Rafe was standing in the grand foyer in an animated conversation with Vincent. Melanie approached.

The two men turned in her direction. A smile moved Rafe's mouth.

"I hope the interview process wasn't too difficult," she said when she came to a stop in front of the duo.

Rafe chuckled. "I was just telling Vincent that your team could get a job with the FBI any day."

Her right brow flickered in amusement. "Yes, they are very good at what they do."

"I'm looking forward to seeing who you'll come up with to fit the bill."

Melanie extended her hand. "We'll be in touch."

He clasped her hand in his. "I'll give you a call when I get back to New York—in about a week."

"Fine. Safe travels."

He released her hand and Vincent walked him to the door, clapping him heartily on the back before returning to the women.

"Should we meet now?" Jessica asked, "Or do we

want to wait until tomorrow?" She looked from one face to the other.

"We may as well run through everything now and make our decision," Melanie said, knowing that her real motivation was that she could rationally convince herself that Claude—and Rafe for that matter—were clients and nothing more. Some other woman's dream come true. She inhaled deeply and released a breath of resolve. "Let's do this."

Claude let his Harley rev down to a soft purr and coasted into his Westchester estate driveway. It wasn't often that he had a chance to ride, take his bike out and run her full throttle. But when opportunity presented itself, he took it.

There was a lone light coming from the ground-floor window of his two-story Tudor. His housekeeper, Lin, always left a light on when she knew he'd be coming home. The small gesture took some of the edge off of coming home to an empty house. The upside was he generally was only here maybe two weeks out of the month. The rest of the time he was either in Albany or in D.C., where the work and rigorous hours ensured his being alone. There were women. There were always women to take the chill off of lonely nights. But he had yet to find someone that he wanted to be with beyond a few meals at great restaurants and uncomplicated sex. In his world it took a certain kind of woman to understand the demands of his life. So for the most part he kept his relationships few and far between. It was simpler that way.

After changing into his workout clothes, he went downstairs to his home gym in the basement, loaded with the latest exercise equipment that could easily rival the most upscale gym.

He put in at least an hour three days per week. It not only kept him in peak physical condition, but also kept his mind sharp and his hormones at a manageable level. After a good workout and a hot shower, Claude settled down in front of the television and tuned into his favorite news show, MSNBC. Rachel Maddow was interviewing the Health and Human Services Secretary on the health reform bill.

He leaned back and tried to focus on the discussion, but his thoughts kept drifting back to his afternoon in Sag Harbor. Jessica and Veronica didn't leave a pebble unturned during the interview. They'd all but taken notes about his life starting in the womb. He chuckled at the memory and wondered who they would find for him. What woman would be his perfect match? *Someone like Melanie Harte*, a distant voice whispered in his head. *She would be ideal. Beautiful, intelligent, sexy, well-traveled and powerful in her own right—a devastating combination*. He wondered if Melanie had a man in her life, and if so, what was he like? What did he do for a living? And the million dollar question: How did she feel about him?

A sudden clap of thunder startled him out of his mind games and none too soon. His imagination was on the verge of taking him someplace he didn't need to go. Melanie Harte was not an option.

Claude crossed the room to the window and closed it. He stood in front of the arched panes of glass as the heavens lit up with a burst of brilliant white light, illuminating the sky.

The ringing phone drew his attention from the spectacle of light. He picked up the phone from the end table and recognized the cell number right away.

"Traci…how are you?"

Her laughter filled the phone lines. "Don't you simply hate technology and what it has done to the element of surprise? I'm fine. Better than fine and I'm in town for a few days. I was hoping we could get together if you're going to be around."

"Where are you staying?"

"The Marriott in midtown. Lucked out and got a suite."

He and Traci had met about five, six years earlier when he was at the U.N. conference with the senator. Traci was an attaché and spent most of her time traveling, as well. Never married, career politico with aspirations to run for office. Smart, easy on the eyes and low maintenance.

Claude glanced at the clock. Almost eight. He listened to the ping of the rain bouncing off the windows. An hour drive into the city and then back. What the hell. He could use some uncomplicated company. "Late dinner?"

"Sounds great. I'll meet you in the bar whenever you get here. The restaurant closes at eleven but… room service is available until two."

Her offer was clear. If he decided to stay, it wouldn't be a problem.

"I'll see you soon." He hung up the phone and prepared for the rest of his night.

Claude strode into the lobby of the Marriot shortly after nine-thirty. As usual for midtown Manhattan hotels, the lobby, the bar and the restaurant were pulsing with activity. He slipped out of his black linen jacket and draped it over his arm as he wound his way around the bustling bodies and headed in the direction of the bar.

He spotted her before she saw him. Her fiery red hair with sunset highlights was like a beacon, falling in a tumble of silken waves to her bare shoulders. She wore black, as he did. Her snuggly fitted dress hugged every inch of her, at least the few inches that were covered by fabric. She was in an animated conversation with a man who seemed intent on discovering what she may have hidden between her very inviting cleavage that rose above the scoop neck top of her dress.

Claude smiled. Traci was still being her devilish self. He moved into her line of sight and when she spotted him, her emerald-green eyes lit up like fireworks. She put down her glass, patted her conversation companion on the shoulder and walked away, leaving him with his mouth hanging open.

"Claude." She walked right up to him, slid her arms around his neck and kissed him full on the lips.

He hooked one arm around her narrow waist and pulled her tight against him for a quick trip down memory lane before breaking the kiss. "I would ask how you're doing, but I can tell you're doing just fine."

Traci laughed and linked her fingers with Claude's. "Girl has to have some fun. I'm starved. How about you?"

He thought of the plate Lin had fixed and left in the oven that he'd never had a chance to touch. "Me, too."

"Good. Come on."

"So, catch me up. How is life in the fast lane?" Traci asked as she cut into her steak.

"Well, you know the senator has his hands in as many pots as the law allows. He's chair of two major committees and sits on a half dozen others. My plate stays full." He chewed on his forkful of steak, which nearly melted in his mouth.

"Do you think it was the job or the whole black, white thing that kept us from getting together?" Traci asked casually.

Claude drew in a breath in concert with the rise and fall of his brows. "Hard to say. Maybe a little of both."

"Or maybe," she wagged her fork at him, "we were both living out some jungle fever fantasy. Know what I mean?"

Claude chuckled. "Maybe you're right," he said, adding to the repartee.

"But the truth is, neither one of us was or is ready to slow down."

Claude chose not to comment. He sipped from his glass of wine.

"Hey, did you get to the embassy party the other night? I know you don't usually attend, but I heard this was a good one, as embassy parties go."

Claude's thoughts flashed back to that night and meeting Melanie for the first time. Now that's the kind of woman he would consider slowing down for.

Traci was waving her hand in front of his face. "Earth to Claude."

He blinked the image away.

"Where'd you go?"

"Sorry…just thinking about the party. Yes, it was nice, great food, music…" His voice drifted off.

Traci angled her head to the side and tucked her palm beneath her chin. "Who is she?" Her eyes gleamed in the light.

Claude leaned back and wiped his mouth with the napkin. "Why must there be a she?"

"There's always a she…or a he when someone gets that look in their eyes."

"Really?" he said, deadpan.

"Scientific fact. So, come on, tell."

"There's nothing to tell."

She gave him a skeptical look. "Hmm. Then you're free and clear to spend the night with me, like old times," she said, a hint of challenge in her voice.

Had it been a week ago he wouldn't have hesitated. It was crazy to think that something could go on between him and Melanie. They barely knew each other. Not to mention that he'd laid down twenty-five big ones. The only thing between them was business. He focused on Traci. She was beautiful, fun, smart and hot as a volcano. He reached across the table and took her hand. "If I tell you this, you have to swear you won't laugh."

"If it's funny, I'm going to laugh," she said, totally serious.

Claude threw up his hands. "Okay, forget it."

Traci surged forward. "Okay, okay. I won't laugh. I swear." She crossed her heart and stared at him with wide-eyed innocence.

Claude stared her down for a minute, drew in a breath and debated about what he was on the verge of saying. He linked his fingers together. "I went to a dating service."

Her mouth opened but Claude's warning glare kept anything from coming out.

"I'm not talking about some online stuff. It's classy, high tech and cost fifty grand to get on board." He went on to explain what had transpired and how it was Alan's idea to find someone for him.

"Alan Harte? You're kidding. Mr. Footloose and Fancy Free?"

Claude laughed. "Yes, him. His sister Melanie runs the family business." Just saying her name made his stomach jump. He went on to tell her about The Platinum Society, how it operates and their money-back guarantee.

Traci was genuinely fascinated. "The Platinum Society, huh?" She twisted her lips in concentration, then turned her focus on Claude. "It all sounds fantastic, but why are you doing this? It's so out of character for you."

"That's what I kept telling myself. But the truth... I'm getting tired of looking to the future and the only one in the picture is me."

"I should be hurt and insulted," Traci said, "that I'm not even in consideration."

"Traci...I..."

She held up her hand to ward off an explanation that wouldn't change anything. "I'm a realist, Claude. I know what goes on between us does not a forever make. I'm fine with that. You deserve someone, someone special." She lifted her wine glass. "To The Platinum Society and finding the perfect woman for a perfect man."

They touched glasses.

"You think maybe if I got a serious tan?" she teased and they both fell into laughter.

Claude opted not to stay the night, but they did spend a few hours over dessert and drinks catching up on Capitol Hill gossip, unrest in the Middle East and the ridiculousness of airport security, to which Claude declared, "Before it's all over we're going to be down to our birthday suits going through airport security."

"Hopefully not before I leave for Turkey," she said over her laughter as they prepared to depart. "I'm heading out next week."

Traci walked with him to the entrance of the hotel, where they shared a hug and kiss for the road, and as he lay in bed that night, alone, he could have kicked himself for not taking Traci up on her generous offer as nature and hormones conspired against him. He turned onto his side. Hopefully, TPS was as good as they claimed. Then maybe he could stop turning down beautiful, willing women and get his mind off of Melanie.

Chapter 5

"These are the two that I came up with for Mr. Montgomery," Veronica said as she pressed a button on the remote to activate the video projector. "The first is Dayna Grant. She runs several art galleries/lounges along the East Coast," Veronica said. "She's thirty-three, five foot eight, one hundred and thirty eight pounds, divorced, no children. She has an MBA from Stanford and loves to travel."

Melanie made some notes as she listened to Dayna talk about herself in the interview and what she was looking for in a man.

"And then I thought that Grace Freeman was also a good choice. She's not as high-powered as Dayna, but she can hold her own. I've seen her work a room during one of her book launch parties. She has class and style to match Mr. Montgomery."

"Yes, I remember her. Really nice woman. I liked her a lot." Melanie continued to make notes. Either of these women would be perfect for Claude, certainly on paper. The real test would come once they'd met and had gone out a time or two.

The screen darkened. Veronica turned to her aunt. "So what do you think?"

"I think you're very good at what you do," she said, her gaze glimmering with pride.

"Thanks, Aunt Mel."

"Get it set up. And give Max a call at Deity Supper Club."

"In Brooklyn?"

Melanie grinned. "Yes, take them both out of their element. Deity is super classy, great food and the drinks are to die for."

Veronica nodded slowly as the idea took hold. "And since we're going off script, how about sending Claude and Grace to Madame X in the Village in Manhattan for a Lady Jane Salon reading?"

Melanie giggled and clapped her hands. "I love it. Perfect. And maybe we can work it out so that Grace can do a reading."

"I'll get right on it." Veronica looked at her aunt.

"We usually do the yacht or fly the couple somewhere. Why the change?"

Melanie paused for a moment, collecting her thoughts. "Generally we make it so easy for the couple on the first date. We set them up in the lushness of what they are used to." She lifted her chin and folded her arms. "I think they need a bit of a challenge. If they can get through it, experience something new, then we can pull out all the stops."

"I'll take care of it."

Melanie nodded. "Keep me posted. Give Mr. Montgomery a call, bring him up to date on what we have for him so far."

"Oh…" The one word from Veronica hung in the air.

"Problem?"

"No, it's just that, well it's what you usually do."

"We're doing things differently, remember?" was all she said and walked out.

Melanie went to her room to change into her running clothes. The air was cool, almost chilly, but her body was on fire. She needed to douse the flames. A run along the beach and around the property always helped to clear her head.

Dressed and ready she told Evan that she was going out for a run in case anyone was looking for her.

She pulled her headband down over her ears and

wrapped a towel around her neck. Her midnight-blue running jacket came just below her hips. Her running pants in the same blue clung to her legs like a second skin.

At the front door, she did several minutes of stretching before taking off. She began slowly, heading down the path from the mansion onto the bluff then to the steps that led down to the beach. The sun was pale today, barely strong enough to give off any rays of warmth. The sky was slightly overcast and storm clouds could be seen in the distance. The water was gray and choppy. She took this all in as she started out on her run. It was a picture of solitude and loneliness, emotions that she was unable to shake lately. And as a result she'd quietly begun to question her ability to manage the business. Between having the hots for her client and questioning her own feelings, she wasn't sure of anything anymore. How effective could she continue to be in helping perfect strangers find love when she couldn't even put together a relationship of her own?

She started off along the beach, following the horizon for about a mile, willing her mind to simply turn off and relax for a few minutes. But her thoughts refused to obey.

The truth was, after Steven, she'd dived into work, putting all that she had into finding love, the kind of love she'd shared with her husband, for others. And for a long time, that was enough. She felt fulfilled. There had been men from time to time, men that she met at parties or while traveling. She'd even received several proposals over the years. Yet there had been no one that made her want to say "I do." She'd seen the rainbow, crossed the colors to the other side, but she never got her pot of gold, her reward.

A low ominous rumble caused her to look outward. The oncoming dark-gray storm clouds sped across the foamy waves. In the distance a zigzag of terrifying bright light cut across the sky. She had maybe five minutes before heaven and earth collided. She picked up her pace and headed back toward the house and none too soon. Halfway there, the first drops of rain began to fall and within moments, it was nearly blinding. If she hadn't run this road a million times she would have never found her way back. The rain splashed against her face, whipped up by the frenzied wind, pinning her clothes to her body, determined, it seemed, to push her away from where she wanted to go. Her legs suddenly weighed a ton as she ran across the sand that sucked her feet like a vacuum. The added exertion accelerated her heart. She wiped water from her eyes as she rounded the bend and could just make out the shape of the house up ahead. If she wanted a workout, she'd certainly gotten one. She reached the steps and fought against the rising wind and rain to make it to the top then across the lawn and down the pathway to the front door, ignoring everything except the refuge of her home.

She came through the door, dripping wet and shivering cold. She stripped out of her jacket, took off her sneakers and walked toward the stairs when the sound of male voices drifted to her from the living room. One she recognized immediately, the second made her pulse race. She quickened her steps in the direction of the stairs and the safety of her bedroom. Just as she zipped by the partially opened door, Alan stepped out.

"There you are. We were getting worried. I was just telling Claude that if you didn't show up in the next two minutes I was coming out to look for you."

Melanie froze. Her nieces and nephew crowded the doorway. Claude stepped out behind her brother. She was mortified.

"I really have to get out of these wet clothes. Then I can talk." She gave Claude a brief smile and it took every ounce of willpower not to run like a rabbit chased by a fox up to her room.

Once behind closed doors she fought back a scream of disbelief. What in the world was Claude doing here? She was going to have a serious talk with her brother. She headed for the bathroom, turned the shower on full blast and peeled out of her dripping wet clothes.

Thunder erupted like dynamite in the sky, rattling the windows. The lights flickered for a moment then settled.

As she stood under the steaming water she wondered what she could possibly say to her brother: Don't bring Claude here without telling me so that I can be presentable because I have a thing for him, I think?

She held her face up to the water. Of course that was out of the question and ridiculous. Claude was Alan's longtime friend. Both of them were in town and it stood to reason that they would hang out together. In addition to which, this was where Alan's family could always be found.

She sighed, gave her body another lathering then turned off the water. Wrapped in towels, she walked barefoot back into her bedroom. What she wanted to do was curl up under her comforter, sip on a glass of brandy and watch a *Criminal Minds* marathon. None of which she could do without seeming totally rude. Instead she blow dried her hair, lotioned her body and put on a casually fabulous outfit in a silver-toned cotton-knit jersey fabric. The lounging pants and top flowed softly against her skin. Slippers for her feet and a dash of her favorite perfume behind each ear and she was ready. She took a last look in the mirror, then joined her family and guest downstairs.

When she entered the room, Claude was in an animated conversation with Alan about the New York Knicks' latest game. Her nieces and nephew were gone. Heads turned in her direction. Claude stood.

Melanie crossed the room toward him. She extended her hand. "I see my brother has managed to get you all the way out here again and in the middle of a storm no less," she said good-naturedly.

He took her hand and held it. "When a black SUV with tinted windows pulls up in front of your door and a voice from deep in the recesses of the interior says 'get in,' you get in." He chuckled.

"You make it sound sinister," Alan said while he fixed himself a drink at the bar.

"My brother has always fancied himself a spy," Melanie said in a moderately bad attempt at a British accent. "That's why he works at the State Department and no one really knows what he does."

"Very funny." Alan took a sip of his drink.

The lights flickered.

Melanie moaned. "Not a good sign."

"Do you get power outages up here a lot?" Claude asked.

"If we have really bad electrical storms we have been known to lose power for a few minutes or a day or two. Fortunately for us, and most of the town, we have a backup generator. So the problem isn't so much with the homes but getting in and out of town. No lights and the inevitable flooding."

Claude hummed deep in his throat.

"My brother is a lousy host, always has been. Can we get you something to eat, drink?"

"No, I'm fine, thanks."

"Evan should be fixing dinner. But just let me know if you want something beforehand." She turned to her brother. "Were you planning to stay for dinner?"

Before he could answer, the sky lit up and the inside of the house was swathed in darkness.

"The generator should kick in in a minute if the lights don't come back on," Alan offered.

Several moments passed. Voices of concern coming from the hallway drew closer.

"Hey, what's going on with the power?" Vincent asked from the other end of a flashlight. His sister was right behind him.

"The generator should be on by now," Veronica complained.

"Hey where is everybody?" Jessica yelled from the basement, her voice coming closer as she bounded up the stairs.

"We're in here," Vincent replied.

Jessica, a bit breathless, joined the group just as

another bolt of lightning provided the only other illumination.

Alan walked to the window. "This is a bad one. No lights on the entire shore."

"What?" the group chorused in disbelief and joined Alan at the window.

Veronica picked up the phone and brought it to her ear. "Dead."

"What about your cell, Alan?" Melanie asked.

He took his BlackBerry out of his pocket. "Weak but usable. Government has to be good for something." He put it back in his pocket.

Evan entered the room bearing a tray of lighted candles. "I found the hurricane lamps in the cabinets." He set the lamps down, then placed the lighted candles on the tables and shelves around the room.

"Thanks, Evan," Melanie said.

"Fortunately I'd already finished dinner when the lights went out. Should I bring everything in here or should I set up in the dining room?"

Melanie moved away from the window. "In here is fine."

He nodded and walked out.

"Guess we can pretend we're camping," Jessica offered, "like when we were kids."

Veronica and Vincent laughed. "Oh, you mean the times that you used to cry because you were scared of the dark?" Vincent taunted.

"No, I was thinking of the time that you got chased around by a bee all day and it finally bit you on the nose, which blew it up to five times its normal size. And Cheryl Adams wouldn't speak to you for a week. That's more like the time I was talking about," Jessica replied with deadpan sarcasm.

Veronica whooped with laughter. "I remember! You were a mess."

"I'm gonna call my wife," Vincent said. "Someone loves me." He walked over to the corner near the window and took out his phone. Shortly he was in conversation with his wife, assuring her that if at all possible he would get home.

"From the look of it out there, you're going to have to camp out here today, buddy," Alan said to Claude. "The rain isn't letting up."

"You really think so?" His shadow lengthened and shortened in the candle light.

"If nothing else it's too dangerous to drive in weather like this. The chances of flash flooding are almost certain and it's pitch black outside," Melanie said. "We have plenty of room. Don't even worry about it."

Claude inhaled slowly then shrugged. "The locals know best," he conceded, knowing that he had no qualms whatsoever of spending the night under the same roof as Melanie Harte.

Evan rolled the food cart into the room and began

setting out dinner on the long serving table that braced the wall. The silver covered trays couldn't contain the mouth-watering aroma that wafted from under the lids.

Braised baby lamb chops in Evan's special sauce, saffron rice, a mixed greens salad, fresh string beans and fingerling potatoes.

"Enjoy," Evan said before leaving the room.

"I'm going to check the generator. It should have kicked in by now."

Melanie put a gentle hand on Vincent's shoulder. "It can wait. Sit down and eat first. The generator will either come on or it won't."

"You sure?"

"Yes," she smiled. "It'll be fine. Everyone help yourself." She found herself standing behind Claude on the short buffet line. In the semi-darkness she could satisfy her longing to see him without being seen. She felt small in his presence—not tiny or overpowered but rather enveloped. His solid broad back called out to be touched and measured by experienced fingers. The back view was equally as stimulating as the front as her eyes drifted down below the leather belt.

"Can I fix your plate?"

The question jolted her from her sensual meandering. She looked up and he was staring at her and she could make out the hint of a curious smile. Her throat was dry and couldn't put the pieces of a sentence together for a moment. She cleared her throat and her naughty thoughts. "Hum, sure. I'll have what you're having," she said, her wit returning just in time.

Claude picked up a plate and began placing the food on it. He handed it to Melanie before filling his own. They walked together to the window and sat on the padded bench, watching nature have its way as they ate.

"It's really quite humbling to watch this display," he said thoughtfully, as the waves crashed against the shore, their fury spewing out in rabid foam.

"It reminds us of what a small part we play in the grand scheme of things. Sometimes, as much as we may want to rail against 'the forces,' all we can do is stand back and let things happen the way that they should," Melanie replied.

He cut part of his chop and chewed slowly. His dark eyes picked up the flickering lights of the candles and reflected back as he observed her. "You surprise me."

"How is that?"

"I don't know if I would have expected such a philosophical statement from you. I imagined you to be more pragmatic, rational, straightforward."

"Because I run a business?" she asked, curious as to his reasoning.

He nodded. "Yes."

"True this is a business, but it's about people and feelings. Beyond all the high-tech stuff that we do, we have to be sensitive, see beyond all the analytical profiles. What we do is about happiness. There's nothing rational about that."

"You're absolutely right." His gaze settled on her for a moment. She shifted in her seat. "How long have you been involved in the business?"

She told him of her indoctrination by her grandmother and mother a decade ago. "I started this thing never thinking that I would stay or that I would love it as much as I do. There's nothing compared to seeing the joy on the faces of the couples we match up."

"What about you?"

She reached for her glass of wine. Her hand shook ever so slightly and she was grateful for the low light.

"I'm sorry—that's really none of my business."

"No. It's fine. It's not the first time someone has asked—indirectly—how I can run a matchmaking service and not have a love life of my own." She drew in a breath to settle herself inside.

"I was married once," she began. "His name was Steven. We had three glorious years together before he died. Heart attack at thirty-five." She shook her head in the same manner of disbelief she felt ten

years ago. "Perfectly healthy. Went for a run…and…"
She looked away as the memories rushed toward her
on the crests of the waves, unstoppable. Her chest
concaved, hit by the force of the memory of that
day.

Claude took the vibrating glass from her hand and
set it on the sill. "I'm sorry. I had no idea," he said
softly. His hand covered hers and gently squeezed
it.

She blinked several times and willed the air to
move through her lungs. All of her emotions seemed
to have risen to the surface these past few days. It
left her feeling vulnerable and not in control of her
life, a place that she didn't want to be in. After losing
Steven she'd vowed that she wouldn't allow herself
to ever be the victim of anything she didn't have a
hand in. So far she'd won. Until recently. Her outlook
when it came to the couples they matched was one
thing—her personal life was different. At least that's
what she told herself.

"No need to apologize," she said, finding her voice.
She forced a smile. "We didn't get much of a chance
to talk after your interview," she said, switching the
topic from her to him. "I hope it wasn't too awful."

He laughed and she enjoyed the sound.

"It was definitely thorough. I think that they found
out things about me that I didn't know myself."

"What did you discover?"

He leaned back against the frame of the window and angled his head slightly to the side. "Hmm, well for all the public work that I do and interacting with countless people, I'm really a bit of a homebody." He chuckled. "Seems like my perfect evening is a night at home in front of some roaring fire, with my soul mate resting across my lap while I read to her from her favorite novel."

Melanie saw her head resting on his lap as he stroked her hair and his deep, smooth voice brought the pages of Hemingway's *The Sun Also Rises* to life. *Dream on girl.* "I think that's a great image."

"Do you?"

His gaze was so personal that it took the simple question to that place in her soul she didn't want to address. Especially not with him.

"Aunt Mel."

Vincent's approach saved her from making a fool of herself. She turned toward him.

"I checked out the generator. Looks like a bad fuse. We won't be getting any power from it any time soon."

"Thank for checking, sweetie. We'll have to call the company in the morning."

"I already called. Left a message, so hopefully we'll get a call back first thing in the morning."

"Nothing we can do about it until then except get comfortable for the night. Thanks," she said again.

Vincent nodded and returned to the buffet. She blew out a breath of frustration before turning to Claude. "Looks like you'll be spending the night."

"It's getting to be a better idea every minute."

A flutter like butterfly wings stirred her deep and low. Her ears burned. "Whenever you're ready I can…get someone to show you your room. It will be at the top of the stairs to your left. And—"

"What do you like to read?" he asked, effectively throwing her off balance.

"What?"

"There are books everywhere in the house, at least the parts that I've seen. So, what are your favorites?"

She lowered her head and laughed lightly before daring to look back at him. "I have quite a few actually, depending on my mood. I helped my mother and grandmother build the library, so the collection is quite eclectic."

"I can tell that from what I've seen. But you didn't really answer my question."

"Hmm, well, I love the pace of a good mystery. James Patterson and Patricia Cornwell. I've finally been able to get my head wrapped around Toni Morrison and I will always love work from the masters, Hemingway, Baldwin, Marquez, Ellison, Dumas." She shrugged lightly. "And of course, being a provocateur of romance, a steamy romance novel is always nearby."

"Of course. Can I refill your drink?"

"I should be asking you that. I'm being a terrible hostess." She hopped down from the sill. "What are you drinking?"

"Wine is fine."

"Sure you don't want something stronger?"

His eyes ran down her body for a hot second. "I don't think that would be a good idea."

She didn't dare respond, at least not to that statement. "I'll be right back."

"You two seem to be getting along rather well," Alan commented under his breath, sidling up to her next to the bar. He refilled his drink.

Her head jerked up. "What's that supposed to mean?"

He held up his hand in defense. "It's not supposed to mean anything. Just an observation. Relax, sis."

She shook her head. "I'm sorry. This whole blackout thing has me off balance."

He draped his arm around her shoulder and pulled her close. "You off balance? Come on, be for real. You always have everything under control."

"Yeah, I do, don't I?" she said with little conviction. It certainly didn't feel like it.

Chapter 6

Evan came into the room and began removing the dishes and dinner trays.

"Let me help with that," Melanie said, putting down the bottle of wine to stack some of the dishes on the rolling cart.

"You're not going to try to get home tonight, are you Evan?" Alan stated more than asked.

"No, I'm going to stay."

"Good." Melanie patted his shoulder. "And don't even think about trying to clean up the kitchen in the dark. I know how you are."

"I guess it can wait, but you know how I hate a messy kitchen."

"Tonight is an exception."

He blew out a breath of resignation. "Just this one time." He pushed the loaded cart out of the door to the kitchen.

Melanie finished fixing the two glasses of wine and was about to return to her spot by the window.

"I think he likes you."

"Who?"

"Who do you think?"

She glanced a look in Claude's direction. His body was silhouetted in stark relief against the pane of the window. "Don't be ridiculous. He's a client and I'm being hospitable. Nothing more, nothing less."

"Okay," Alan said and she could almost hear the smirk in his voice.

Did she give off a vibe that she wasn't aware of? Or was her brother doing to her what he'd been doing since they were kids—messing with her head? That had to be it.

She returned with the drinks and handed Claude his.

"Thanks." He took a sip. "I've been sitting here watching this storm, the power and shape that it takes, the things that it does to the horizon. It's incredible to look at."

She sat back down and stared out into the turbulent night. The only thing to be seen was the white suds of the waves as they pummeled the shore and the outlines of homes and rocks when lightning took their instant picture.

"It is pretty awesome." She took a sip of her drink. "What about you? Tell me something that isn't in your bio and profile."

He chuckled. "What could they have missed? Oh, I got a B in spelling in second grade."

Melanie's laughter floated back and forth between them. "Yeah, I have a feeling we didn't go back quite that far." She paused a moment, knowing that she was treading on shaky ground, but she appeased herself with the notion that she was doing this as part of getting to know her client. It was in everyone's best interest. "Let me put it this way. Since I haven't gone over all the information, why don't you tell me what you think you want me to know?"

"Hmm. I'll skip over to all the good stuff," he said, making her laugh, and she realized he made her laugh often and easily.

He talked a little bit about his job, what he liked and disliked about being chief of staff for the senator. He told her about his love of fishing, which he rarely got to do, and his motorcycle, which he rode whenever he could.

"I can see you on a bike," she said with renewed appreciation for this man's man.

"Yeah, it's pretty cool," he said, bobbing his head. He looked across the room and zeroed in on the piano.

"Come on." He took her hand and walked her over to the piano. He sat down on the bench and invited her to join him. Once she was settled, he drifted into a rendition of "Ordinary People," then segued to "A House is Not a Home," then a medley of some jazz pieces and R&B favorites. Everyone from their spot in the room either hummed or sung along, and for a time lost themselves in the moment and the music.

"That was amazing," Melanie enthused when he brought his one-man show to an end. "If you ever leave government, you can always get a night club gig."

"I'll keep that in mind."

When they looked up, they realized that they were alone. The others had drifted off.

"Well," Melanie said on a breath, "I should show you to your room."

"Sure."

They pushed back from the bench. Claude's arm braced her back when she stumbled over the leg of the bench. She turned halfway and found herself in an almost embrace.

Her cheeks heated and again she was thankful for the darkness.

"Good catch. Thanks." She righted herself and moved out of his arms and realized how good they felt around her, even better than they did the night they met.

She went to the other side of the room and took one of the lamps and a flashlight from the table. She handed the lamp to Claude and led the way upstairs with the flashlight.

When they reached the top of the landing Melanie turned left down the hallway, adorned on either side by abstract art from a local female artist from the Harbor who'd captured Melanie's attention.

"Your room is right here." She opened a door and, even in the dim light, Claude could see it was a stunning layout. King-sized bed, bay windows overlooking the surf, flat-screen television mounted on the wall, lush carpet cushioned any footfall. An armoire and an eight-drawer dresser provided the additional furnishings, along with a deep, overstuffed lounge chair near the window.

"This is some spread for a guest," he said.

Melanie laughed lightly. "We never know who might wind up staying with us and we want to make sure that everyone is as comfortable as possible. During the summer months we have guests that stay for a couple of weeks at a time. It's quite beautiful here in the summer."

"Yes, it is." He drew in a long breath and slowly exhaled.

The awkward moment introduced itself and stood between them. Waiting.

Claude cleared his throat.

Melanie lightly ran her tongue across her bottom lip. "Um, the bath is through that door," she managed to say.

He nodded but didn't speak, his gazed fixed on her, taking her in.

If anyone would have asked her what in the world she was thinking at that moment, she would not have been able to explain. It was like watching a movie. That fateful moment when the two actors realize that they can't deny their attraction any longer and the woman finds herself tightly woven in the embrace of the man she's desired but couldn't have.

Their kiss was surreal and electric, inevitable yet stunning in its suddenness. Warmth became a physical thing touching and stroking her curves, stoking what before was smoldering until her skin was on fire and the pool of heat settled in her center.

His mouth was more than she'd imagined when she memorized the dip and thickness of his lips. It was firm and soft and full and gentle and teasing and commanding—all at once. She couldn't keep up with the sensations so she let herself become one with them.

"I've thought about this from the day that I met you," he said against the hollow of her neck.

The feathering of his lips along the lines of her throat vibrated through her body. She moaned softly, sinking further into his embrace, tracing the sinewy lines of his broad back with the balls of her fingers. He eased her closer to the hard contours of his body until they were molded together as perfect as an artist's sculpture.

They seemed to think and feel the same thing simultaneously as they moved in unison toward the bed that beckoned them. Sitting on the edge, Claude eased back and looked closely at Melanie. He caressed her cheek and cupped her chin in his hand when she placed her lips there. He stroked her shoulder, moving slowly down her arm. "Is this what you want?"

Her eyes fluttered open. She focused on the sincerity in his gaze that struggled with the passion that hovered there.

"Yes, I want this," she said in whispered conviction.

He took her mouth then, melding it with his before removing her top and tossing it aside. Her full breasts rose to greet the heat of his lips, which brushed tantalizingly across the butter-soft crests.

Melanie shuddered as the raw thrill shot through her. He reached behind her and unsnapped her bra, then eased the straps over her shoulders. In the play of shadow and light he tried to memorize how perfect she was. He took her hand and gently pulled her to her feet. He unfastened the one button of her slacks and slid them down over her hips.

She couldn't remember the last time she felt so beautiful through the eyes of someone else. He grazed the pad of his thumbs lightly across the hard ridges of her nipples and her inner thighs trembled, the hot silky dew slid along her insides, readying her body for him.

With sure fingers she began unbuttoning his shirt. He tugged it off and tossed it next to her clothing on the floor. He didn't give her a chance to undress him further—he did it all.

Melanie's soft inhale at the sight of him fueled his own desires. They stretched out on the bed, exploring each other, slow and deliberate then with more urgency as their needs blossomed. His lips, his tongue, his fingertips acted as a conductor, a maestro stirring her flesh, her mind, the very blood that coursed through her body setting it all on fire.

She found herself beneath him, his weight like a comforting quilt that she wanted to wrap herself up and around in.

The thickness and heat of his erection pressed against her and instinctively she parted her thighs to give him what they both longed for.

He was so incredibly hard, she thought in an instant of clarity, which only intensified the warm liquid that slipped out to meet him.

Claude pushed just the head against her opening

and his head spun. She whimpered ever so softly as he slid his arms beneath her to lift her flush against him.

She spread her thighs wider and bent her knees as he pushed past her throbbing opening. They both moaned at the exquisite rush of pleasure that shot through them as he moved deep and slow within her.

Claude groaned almost in a kind of agony, the feeling so intense that it shook him down to the balls of his feet and all he wanted to do was be still and let it wash through him. But need overrode all else and he moved in and out of her, hoping to touch and claim every inch within her.

He wasn't just inside of her, his mouth and hands made love to her, as well. He kissed, he nibbled, he touched, he suckled, every act, driving her to a near frenzy.

Melanie longed for the magnificent release that she knew was close at hand, but she didn't want the ecstasy to stop. It was too sweet, too perfect. But she could feel herself on the brink of coming. It began in the back of her legs, the heat, the tingling, moved up her thighs and taunted her undulating behind, settled in her center and grew like a firestorm, building, uncontrolled.

He was moving faster now, deeper, stronger.

She tightened her knees along the sides of his body. Her heart was racing out of control, her breath coming in short escalating pants as her fingers dug into his back, her face buried in his neck to stifle her cries of release that slammed into her like the waves that crashed against the bluffs below the window.

Her body was electrified as jolt after jolt rocketed through her, shaking her like a rag doll with its power. But he wasn't done. Even as her insides continued to grip and release him, he moved steadily in and out of her, his erection even harder and more full if that was even possible.

Claude slid his arm under her hips, his other behind her back pulling her tight until they were sealed together from their lips to their toes and he exploded within her, setting her off on another body-rocking climax.

"Oh my God," she whispered against his damp neck.

Their hearts banged and slammed against one another even as the last drops of his essence jerked out of him.

By degrees their breathing slowed, their limbs loosened and their pulses moved toward normal.

Claude kissed her tenderly as if for the first time. So sweet that it brought tears to her eyes.

Cocooned in the security of darkness, they drifted off to a satiated sleep, tucked in each other's arms.

* * *

She wasn't sure how long she'd slept or what woke her. She tried to focus in the dark. Her stomach lurched when it hit her where she was and what she had done. She felt sick. She turned her head slightly. Claude was stretched out next to her. His arm was draped possessively across her waist. Gently and quietly, she lifted his arm and slipped out of bed. In the darkness she located her clothes and got dressed the best she could. With her shoes in her hand she eased toward the door and prayed that she wouldn't run into anyone in the hallway en route to her room.

She closed the door as softly as she could and hurried to her room, where she spent the rest of the night in misery.

Chapter 7

Claude stirred. It was the silence that awakened him. The storm had ceased and the pale moon struggled behind an army of clouds for recognition. The candles were all but burned out, their remains like fallen clothing at their bases. He turned, anticipating the warmth of Melanie's body, and met cool emptiness. He sat up, adjusting his eyes to the gray light.

He tossed the twisted sheet aside and noticed the digital bedside clock flashing 2:00 a.m. The power must have come back on while they slept, he rationalized abstractly. He stood and listened for signs of Melanie, thinking that she must be in the adjoining bathroom. On the floor where he'd tossed their clothing, only his remained. He drew in a long breath of reality followed by a mental marathon of questions that ran in succession, never waiting for answers. Why did she leave without saying anything? How did he not hear her? Had something else happened that caused her to leave without explanation?

He reached down on the floor and retrieved his boxers. He couldn't very well go looking for her in the middle of the night, he thought, putting them on, or go knocking on her bedroom door, not that he knew which door it was, and in any case neither scenario was an option. He dropped down onto the side of the bed, then fell back against the firm mattress, throwing an arm across his eyes. What he felt inside was gray like the light beyond his window, affording the viewer just enough illumination to determine shapes and not much more. It didn't feel right at all. But there wasn't a damned thing he could do about it until he saw Melanie again.

Melanie showered and dressed, wanting to extend her morning ritual throughout the day and into the night. Perhaps by then Claude would have gone back with Alan to the city and she wouldn't have to face him. The muscles in her throat tightened as she struggled not to cry. How could she have been so stupid, so reckless to jeopardize the business and its reputation just so that she could live out her fantasy of getting laid by Claude Montgomery? Oh God. She was just as trifling as some of the women TPS had refused to deal with.

How could she face her brother, her family knowing what she'd allowed to happen? It would be all over her face. She knew it.

She ran a comb through her hair as she faced the mirror and was appalled at the dark circles under her eyes. There was only so much magic makeup could do. She took her time covering up her indiscretion.

Voices from downstairs reached up to her and she tried to listen for Claude's voice among the others but she didn't hear it. Maybe that was a good thing. Maybe he'd gone. Maybe last night didn't really happen. But it did, you fool.

Tossing the comb on the dresser, she sealed her emotions behind a façade of professionalism when she entered the dining room, although last night was anything but professional.

Evan was at the serving table pouring a glass of juice. Veronica and Jessica were in conversation. Vincent, Alan and Claude were not there. A momentary sensation of relief was quickly replaced by disappointment when Jessica told her that Alan had driven Claude back into the city and Vincent went home to check on Cherise.

Was he that eager to get away from her that he couldn't bother to say goodbye? Maybe she had no reason to feel guilty. Maybe it was no more to him than a roll in the hay. The thought stung.

"You okay, Aunt Mel?" Veronica asked.

Melanie blinked her into focus. She forced herself to smile. "Yes, I'm fine. I didn't sleep very well."

"At least the power is back on," Veronica said. "I have tons of work to do. I told Mr. Montgomery about our choices for him and he seemed very pleased. I'll make the calls today and get everything set up."

Every word was a blow. *He seemed very pleased.* Of course he did. What happened between them was just a fling between two consenting adults. He can walk off without a care in the world, while she was left feeling like the neighborhood good-time girl. She felt ill. She'd never done anything so reckless before. Oh my God…they hadn't used protection.

"Aunt Mel, what is it?" Veronica said, alarm present in her voice. She was halfway out of her seat.

Melanie concentrated on slowing down her racing heart with measured breaths.

"You gasped like you'd seen something horrible."

She did. Herself. She turned her back to her nieces, reached for the coffee on the table and came face to face with Evan.

"You don't look well, Ms. Harte. Maybe I should fix you some tea."

"Thank you. I think that might help."

"Right away."

"Are you coming down with something? You did say you didn't sleep well. Maybe you're catching a cold."

"Maybe. I think I'll take it easy today, just in case," she said, happy for an excuse to steal away to her room.

"We can handle everything here," Jessica offered. "Go rest. I'll ask Evan to bring your breakfast."

Melanie waved off the offer. "Tea is fine for now. Maybe something a little later. Thanks." She walked out of the room and upstairs. It took all she had not to burst into tears.

Quietly she shut her bedroom door. She had no reason to feel so miserable. But she did. She felt silly and she had to get over it. Claude Montgomery may have been her heart and body's desire, but he was still a paying client and she could not, even for a moment, allow him to think that his 50k bought any side favors from her.

What must he think of her? That sick sensation rolled in her stomach again. She shook her head. She would have to put it out of her mind, find a way to mentally move through it and do what she was hired to do: find the perfect woman for Claude Montgomery.

Asking for a refund would be petty, Claude thought as he donned his helmet and pushed his bike down the pathway of his house toward the street. He'd tried to sleep. That was useless. His mind became filled with images and sounds of Melanie and their incredible night together. Only it all seemed like something he'd made up, a figment of his imagination. He certainly couldn't talk to his best friend, Alan, about the situation. "Oh, by the way, bro, I slept with your sister last night and it was fabulous." Had it been any other woman, he was sure that Alan would have some great advice along with a hearty congratulatory slap on the back. But this was his sister and it was clear from how he talked about her, talked to her and treated her that he truly adored Melanie.

This wasn't his fault, he reasoned as the mighty engine roared to life beneath him. But of course it was. He'd kissed her first. Told her it was what he wanted from the moment they'd met. So what if it was true? Had he not kissed her, become tantalized by her lips, her scent, the feel of her next to him, beneath him, wrapped around him, then the fact that she was gone without a word when he awoke wouldn't matter. He wouldn't give a damn. And he was mad as hell at himself that he cared.

He took off down the street, heading for the highway. He had no particular destination in mind, he only knew that he needed to get out, find a way to clear his head. He raced past cars on the highway, weaving in and out of traffic, eliciting the blare of horns and strings of curses from the drivers. He didn't care. He could feel his anger, humiliation and disappointment boil beneath the surface. How had she been able to get under his skin so quickly and so thoroughly to a point where he wasn't thinking clearly? He'd never been one of those guys that was led by their little head. So why now, and why Melanie Harte?

He drove further into the Westchester suburbs until the houses became less numerous, guarded by massive lawns, towering trees and electronic gates.

On the ride back from Sag Harbor he'd been withdrawn, unusually quiet with the man he'd known for most of his adult life. When Alan questioned him, he passed it off as being tired, which wasn't as much of a lie as it was a detour from the truth. He was tired after having stayed up the balance of the night wondering what went wrong. What he wanted to talk about was Melanie. He wanted to ask Alan what were the things that made her happy, why had she never married again, was she seeing anyone, what was her favorite dessert, her passion. He wanted to learn everything there was to learn about her, but he couldn't ask, and now he would never know. And that was his last thought before he heard the sound of sirens.

"He's coming around."

The words were filtered through cotton, absorbing

and distorting them. He tried to focus, but concentration was impossible with the pounding in his head and the bright lights shining in his eyes. His entire body throbbed.

"Mr. Montgomery, can you hear me?"

He tried to speak. His mouth felt funny. "Yes," he managed to whisper, his voice harsh and raspy.

"Do you know what happened to you?"

The pounding in his head intensified. He tried to remember. A deer. A deer had appeared on the road just as he'd turned the curve. He hit the brakes and swerved to avoid hitting it and possibly killing them both. The images of falling down into the ravine came in snatches like snapshots. Just glimpses.

He closed his eyes. He ran his tongue over his teeth. *Still there.*

"You're a very lucky man," the doctor was saying. "You have a concussion and two bruised ribs. No broken bones. No internal injuries. It would have been a different story if you'd hit that deer or if your bike had fallen on you. We've given you something for the pain and we're going to observe you overnight. If everything is clear, you can be discharged tomorrow. We'll take another CAT scan to be sure. Get some rest."

He tried to move, but his body ached too much. Did the doctor know what he was talking about, because he sure felt like something was broken, a lot of somethings.

"What some people will do for attention."

Gingerly, Claude turned his head in the direction of the voice and squinted against the fluorescent light.

"Traci?"

"To the rescue."

"But…how did you know I was here?"

"Apparently I was the last number that you dialed on your cell. I guess from the night we had dinner, when you called to say you were on your way." She drew closer to the bed and braced her arms across the railing and looked down at him. "I'm glad they called me."

"I thought you were out of the country."

"Postponed." She ran a finger across his brow. "I called Alan. He said he would get in contact with the senator."

The mention of Alan immediately brought his sister to mind, which was the last thing he needed to do—think about Melanie. Thinking about her is what got him laid up in a hospital bed.

"The doctor said you'll be having headaches for a while and that you'll need to take it easy for at least a week."

The way he was feeling he didn't think forever would be enough time.

"So, with that in mind…" She bent down and lifted up a Louis Vuitton carryall. "I won't take no for an answer, so don't bother to say anything. I'm staying with you for a week. I know you have Lin, but she's not me. I can look after you and I swear," she held her hand over her heart, "I'll stay in the guest room."

He started to laugh and caught himself as his ribs burned from the effort. He swallowed down the pain. "You don't have to do this."

"I know. I want to."

"Can't talk you out of it?"

"No."

He drew in a shallow breath. "Fine." He smiled. "Thanks."

She leaned over the rail and kissed him lightly on the forehead. "Anything for you, sweetie."

Claude took her hand and brought it to his lips. That's the image that Melanie captured when she walked into the room.

Chapter 8

Alan loudly cleared his throat. "Looks like you're already on the mend," he said entering the room, holding Melanie's hand.

"Maybe we should come back," she whispered to her brother, who ignored her and gently pulled her along.

"Traci, I'm so glad that you called me." He walked over to her and kissed her lightly on the cheek. "Traci, this is my sister Melanie. Traci and Claude go way back," he said, oblivious to the tension in the air.

So this was her. And from the look in Claude's eyes, she's more than the owner of that dating service. Traci extended her hand. Something green, like bile seeped through her veins. "Nice to meet you."

"You, too." She turned her attention to Claude. "How are you feeling?"

Claude could barely think straight. What was Melanie doing here? "Like I drove my bike into a ditch," he finally managed to say. A lance-like pain shot through his head. He winced with agony.

Traci immediately leaned over. "Are you okay, baby? You want me to call the nurse back?"

"Naw," he said, taking slow, deep breaths as the pain slowly abated. "They'll just shoot me up with more drugs. I don't want that."

"I don't blame you, buddy. If you can grit through it, that's the best thing. You don't want to have to rely on painkillers."

"But if it gets too bad, don't let your machismo make you suffer," Traci said, stroking his brow.

Melanie wanted to run out of the room. She couldn't stand the sight of the two of them together. Alan said that "they went way back." How damned far? It was clear that they were more than friends. If she felt sick before, there was no word to describe how she felt now.

When she'd gotten the call from Alan that Claude had been in an accident, everything stood still. For an instant she couldn't breathe or ask the question she dreaded: How bad was it? She didn't even remember telling Alan that she would ride with him to the hospital, a two-and-a-half hour drive. She was sure that Alan had been talking to her for most of the trip, but she couldn't tell a soul what he said. She could only imagine the worst. But it was obvious that he was getting all the care he needed. She wanted to leave. Now.

"So Melanie, I've known your brother for years. I'm surprised we haven't met before, especially with both of us knowing Claude." She turned adoring eyes on him.

"Well, people say it's a small world but sometimes it's bigger than we think."

Traci's laugh was musical. "That is true." She continued stroking Claude's hand.

Melanie cringed inside.

"How long are they going to keep you here, man?" Alan asked.

"They're going to take some tests in the morning. If I can get the all clear, I'll be discharged."

"But he'll have to take it easy for a little while. He didn't tell you that he has a serious concussion and several bruised ribs." She glanced at Melanie. "He'll be in good hands. I told him that I was going to stay with him a few days. A housekeeper is fine, but at times like this he needs a personal touch." She smiled.

"I couldn't agree more," Melanie said. "He's lucky to have you."

"Well I had to see for myself that you were all right. When Traci called me, I didn't know what to think."

Traci called? She was the person that Claude contacts in the event of an emergency? Then she was important, they were close. Melanie pressed her lips together to keep from screaming. If things weren't clear before, they were now. She had no reason to keep beating herself up. He used her just like she used him. End of story. Except that he had someone waiting in the wings to fill any gaps. She didn't.

"Thanks for coming, Alan and Melanie." He briefly looked at her. "I really appreciate it." He yawned. "Hmm, 'scuze me. Meds are kicking in." His eyes fluttered closed, then opened again but didn't quite focus.

"The nurse gave him something just before you both arrived," Traci offered.

"We're gonna get out of here and let you get some rest," Alan said.

"Thanks...for comin'," he slurred as the room began to drift in and out of his range of vision.

"He'll be asleep in a minute," Alan said softly. He went around the side of the bed and kissed Traci on the cheek. "Take care of my man. You need anything, just call. I'll probably stop out to see him after he gets home and settled."

"Great. I'll tell him. Call and let me know when you're coming. I'll fix dinner. Melanie, you're more than welcome to come along," she said, a layer of sarcasm lightly painted her words.

"Thank you. I'll keep that in mind."

Alan put his arm around Melanie's shoulder. "Come on, sis, we have a long drive ahead of us."

Melanie couldn't shake the image of Claude and Traci. The pictures haunted her for the entire ride back to Sag Harbor and throughout the night.

She awoke the following morning with a new attitude. To hell with Claude Montgomery. She had a business to run and a major party to plan.

Claude opened the door to his Westchester home and was greeted by Lin.

"Mr. Montgomery, I was so worried. How are you feeling?"

"Achy, but I'll be fine, Lin. You remember Traci."

"Of course. Good to see you again."

"Traci is going to be staying here for a few days."

"I'll make up the guest room." She hurried off.

"She's still efficient," Traci commented. She'd

hoped to spend her time in Claude's room, but that could come later. "Let's get you settled."

Claude inched his way up the stairs, mindful of his taped ribs. The throb in his head was still there but not as intense as the day before. The doctors said that he would experience headaches from mild to severe for a while and eventually they would disappear. That couldn't happen fast enough, he thought, as he stepped into his bedroom.

"It's pretty much the way I remember," Traci said, setting her bag down near the six-drawer dresser.

"I'm not here often enough to do much with it." He sat down on the side of the bed. The exertion of the ride and climbing the stairs began to take its toll. "I think I'll lie down for a while. If you need anything, Lin can get it for you."

"I'll be fine. I'm sure I can find something to keep myself busy. You get some rest. Can I get you anything?"

"No. Thanks."

"The guest room is still across the hall, right?"

"Yeah."

"Great. See you when you get up. I'll check and see if Lin needs any help." She turned to leave.

"Traci."

She stopped and faced him? "Yes?"

"Thanks."

"Don't be silly. That's what friends are for. Get

some rest." She closed the door quietly behind her and wondered how she could make her short stay last permanently.

Alone, Claude stretched out across the bed and shut his eyes. Without warning, Melanie's face appeared behind his closed lids. He'd wanted to ask her a million questions when she appeared at the foot of his bed like a dream come true. But from her demeanor it was clear that she'd only come out of a sense of duty for a client, not because she cared about him.

He drew in a deep breath—and it cost him as a sharp knife-like pain shot across his body. He groaned as he willed it away. He wished that he could do the same with Melanie. But Traci was here, and according to Veronica and Jessica they had several prospective ladies in waiting. All he had to do was heal and get on with life.

He drifted off into a fitful sleep with his arms wrapped around Melanie and him buried deep inside her incredible warmth.

"What are we going to do about Mr. Montgomery?" Veronica asked at their morning meeting.

"Until he's healed, we'll have to put everything on hold," Melanie said.

"I'll make the calls later today," Jessica said. "We only had tentative dates at Deity and Madame X. So that won't be a problem. And I'll give the ladies a call and bring them up to date."

Melanie nodded. "Rafe Lawson called. He's back in town. Do we have a list of prospects?"

"Several," Veronica said. "As soon as I know his schedule I can get something set up."

"Good." She looked around the table. "Anything else?"

They all said no.

"Okay, let's get to work."

Melanie pushed through her morning and into the afternoon. Having something concrete to do kept her mind off of herself. Although she had periodic bouts of dwelling on Claude and the glorious night they'd spent together, any flame that lingered was stamped out when visions of Traci sprung to mind. What she needed was to be in the company of someone other than herself and her marauding thoughts. She reached for the phone and dialed her best friend, Cynthia Graham.

She and Cynthia had been friends since grad school. She owned an art gallery in town and one in Manhattan. Cynthia's artistic instincts ran counter to Melanie's romanticism, which made for a perfect blend. Cynthia was just the person to put the rug back under Melanie's feet.

Cynthia picked up on the third ring. "CG Gallery, how may I change your life?"

"Hey girl, it's me."

"Mel. I was just thinking about you and the fact that we haven't had a girls' night out in ages."

"Great minds," Melanie said, smiling a real smile for the first time in what seemed like forever. "I was calling to see if you were free tonight for dinner and drinks?"

"Absolutely! I finish up here at seven. Wanna stop by around that time, then we can go by my place so I can change? We can talk on the way."

"Perfect. See you at seven."

Melanie hung up, feeling better already. She put the final touches on the guest list and approved the menu from the caterer. The date was set for the Friday four weeks from now. Invitations would go out in the morning. Her annual party was the event of the season in the Harbor, a tradition begun by her grandmother decades ago. Although it was a herculean task, the outcome was well worth the effort. The guest list always included many of her clients, those who had connected with someone and those still on the prowl, along with her long list of athletes, screen and television friends and political associates. Yes, focusing on the party was exactly what she needed, and an evening spent with her best friend would top off her day.

She shut off her computer and went to her room to get ready to meet Cynthia.

* * *

Cynthia was a devout believer in exercise. Although she lived quite a distance from the gallery, she often walked there, doing her part to reduce her carbon footprint. Melanie was not of the same school of thought. They took her car to Cynthia's house.

"How did you all make out the other night during the power outage?" Cynthia asked as they took the winding road to her house.

"Would you believe that our backup generator didn't work?"

"What? After all the money you paid."

"Exactly." She shook her head even as the memories of that night tried to intrude. "Of course the company that installed it was totally apologetic. Apparently a fuse had blown. What about you?"

Cynthia laughed mischievously. "I was tucked happily away," she said with a wink.

Melanie guessed that it was Michael Quinn. He was Cynthia's latest conquest. He was a young up-and-coming artist who had captured more than Cynthia's artistic eye. So far he'd lasted a little longer than the others, Melanie thought absently. Two months if her calculations were correct.

"What about you? Other than spending the night in total darkness."

"Actually that's what I want to talk to you about."

They pulled to a stop on the paved driveway. Cynthia turned to look at her. "Sounds serious."

"I'm trying not to let it be."

They got out of the car. Cynthia looped her arm through Melanie's. "Whatever it is, we'll work it out." She gave her a warm smile as they walked inside.

Cynthia's home was a total reflection of her eclectic taste. Each room in the three-bedroom, two-story home was decorated in a different style, from antique to ultra modern. The walls were adorned with her own work in addition to several rare pieces from the masters and a Basquiat that Melanie simply loved.

"Grab anything you want from the fridge," Cynthia said, "I'm going to do a quick presto change-o and then we can go."

"Take your time." She wandered over to the stereo system and looked through Cynthia's collection of CDs. She picked out several and put them in the disc player.

She heard the shower overhead and the bathroom door slam shut. She went into the kitchen in search of some fruit juice while she waited. The phone rang.

"Mel!" Cynthia shouted from upstairs. "Get that for me, will you?"

"Okay." She walked over to the phone tucked away on the counter. It was an antique white phone with faux gold trim. She picked up the receiver.

"Hello. Graham residence."

There was a pause on the other end.

"I was calling for Cynthia."

The voice sounded oddly familiar.

"She's busy at the moment. Can I take a message and have her call you back?"

"Sure thing, cher. Can you let her know that Rafe Lawson called and I'll try her a little later?"

For a split second all the air got stuck in the center of her chest. *Rafe Lawson. What in the world was he doing calling Cynthia?*

"Of course."

"Thank you."

Mechanically she hung up the phone. Rafe Lawson? Cynthia was seeing him? When did that happen? She drew in a long breath. She should have told him who she was. That would have shook up his arrogant ass. But what little she did know about Rafe was that he probably would have laughed it off and made her feel like a fool.

She shook her head in sharp disbelief. Of course, she had to tell Cynthia that Rafe was one of her clients and that they were in the process of setting him up. He was worse than she thought he was. Fury brewed in the center of her stomach. Rafe was the consummate player. But her best friend was not going to be one of the notches on his belt. As a matter of fact, she was going to cancel his contract with TPS. They didn't need his business.

She opened the fridge and found a bottle of mango nectar. She twisted off the cap and drank straight from the bottle. *Men.*

By the time they reached the restaurant in the center of town, Melanie was all but bursting.

"What is wrong?" Cynthia asked once they'd been seated. "You look like an overblown balloon, and you've been on edge since we left my house."

Melanie reached for her glass of water and took a long swallow. She set the glass down and leaned forward. "I never got to tell you who was on the phone while you were in the shower."

Cynthia flicked a brow. "Okay, you forgot and so did I. Who was it?"

"Rafe Lawson."

Cynthia's eyes lit up and a smile moved slowly across her mouth. "What did he say?"

"He said he'd try you later."

She tsk tsked. "That Rafe is a real character. He told me he's one of your clients."

Melanie was totally taken aback. "He did?"

"Yes. It's how we got to talking actually. He'd stopped in the gallery when he was here last." She looked up toward the ceiling thoughtfully then back at Melanie. "Hmm, maybe a week or so ago."

That would be about right, Melanie calculated.

"He said his father insisted that he work with TPS but that after meeting you and the others, he actually liked the idea. We talked for a pretty long while. He told me that it was really hard for him to meet women who weren't after him for his money, his family name or his connections, so he'd steered clear of anything serious, but he was willing to give you all a shot." She took a sip of her apple martini. "Now do you want to tell me why you were so upset that he'd called?"

Melanie shook her head. She'd been totally wrong about Rafe. He wasn't what he seemed at all, and she'd gotten sucked into the role he'd mastered. The one she should have been worried about was Claude, who came across as this above-reproach gentleman. She'd been wrong all the way around.

"Mel, talk to me. What is going on? What's the big deal about Rafe calling me? I'm sure it was only about the art that I ordered for him." She reached out and covered Melanie's hand.

"I slept with him."

Cynthia jerked back in surprise. Then she beamed. "Well, damn girl, I don't blame you. If I would have had an extra minute, I might have tried him out myself."

"Not him."

"Oh. Okay. Then who?"

"Claude Montgomery."

Cynthia frowned. "Who is he?"

"A client."

Cynthia's eyes widened in surprise. "You! You're kidding. How in the world did that happen?"

Over dinner Melanie poured it all out from the time she and Claude met, the night they'd spent together right up to her visit to the hospital.

When she was done, Cynthia, who usually had a comeback for everything, was momentarily speechless.

"Don't just sit there staring at me, say something."

"I…I'm trying to get my mind wrapped around this. It's so not you, Mel." She looked at her as if seeing her for the first time. "You're not impulsive. And you definitely don't get involved with your clients." She drew in a breath and took Melanie's hand once again. "So he must be really special," she said softly.

Tears welled in Melanie's eyes. "I thought he was," she said, her words catching in her throat. "But he's not. Apparently."

"Things aren't always as they seem, sweetie. Tonight's phone call from Rafe is a perfect example. Even someone as good as you at what you do can be wrong sometimes. You're human."

"Are you telling me that what I saw at the hospital was all in my mind?"

"I'm saying that it might not be what you think.

You know how women are. Maybe she was testing the waters."

"What if she wasn't?"

"What if she was? And if I remember from what you were telling me, you were the one who slunk out in the middle of the night with no explanation. How do you think he felt?"

Melanie sighed heavily. "It doesn't matter anyway. He's a client. I should have never crossed the line."

"But you did, sweetie, you did."

Chapter 9

"Mr. Lawson is here, Aunt Mel," Jessica said, poking her head in her aunt's open office door.

"I'll be right out."

It had been nearly a week since she'd walked into the hospital room and the conversation she'd had with Cynthia. Although she'd made no effort to change the situation, it wasn't resting as heavily on her heart. She'd see Claude soon enough and by then the dust would have settled and they could have their long overdue talk. In the meantime, she had clients to deal with.

She pushed back from her seat and went into the conference room.

"Mr. Lawson," she greeted.

He grinned at her. "I thought we agreed you would call me Rafe." He crossed the room to where she stood and took her hand, bringing it to his lips. "Good to see you again," he said in an intimate tone that brought to mind everything she'd thought about him. But she'd been wrong, she had to remind herself. His playboy routine was just that—a routine.

She took his hand and led him over to the seating area. "How have you been?"

"Good. Busy. And you?"

"The same. We seem to have a mutual friend."

His brandy-tinted eyes brightened. "Yes. Cynthia. She thinks the world of you, by the way. And so do I," he added in a seductive undertone.

"I hope you don't try to overwhelm her with your southern charm."

He roared with laughter. "Is that what they call it? And all along I thought I was just being social."

Melanie chuckled. "Let me turn you over to Veronica. She has some exceptional ladies lined up for you."

"You wouldn't happen to be on that list, would you?"

Melanie stood and looked down at his upturned face. "I don't mix business with pleasure," she said, going along with the flirty word game.

"Oh, I can guarantee it would be all pleasure," he said, his patois slow and sweet.

She looked into his eyes and saw the playfulness and something else…desire. Was she really that far off base when it came to Rafe, or was she reading something that wasn't there? She was seriously beginning to doubt herself and her judgment. "Veronica is waiting." She led the way out.

A little less than an hour later Rafe stepped out of the media room with Veronica behind him. Melanie was crossing the foyer when they emerged. "Are you pleased with our selections?" she asked.

He grinned. "Not bad," he conceded. "I'm looking forward to meeting them."

"Jessica is going to set the first date up for this weekend."

"Perfect. And as you know everything is taken care of from the limo to the food, entertainment, everything," Melanie said.

"Makes my life easier. If it doesn't work, I can always point my finger this way." He winked at Veronica.

"We rarely make mistakes," Melanie said. "It's usually a matter of having to choose between more than one suitable woman or man than the match being wrong."

"I live to be the exception," he said with a wicked

smile. "Good night, ladies." He walked to the door and out.

"He's a handful," Veronica said softly, her eyes following his progress through the window.

Melanie caught the note of longing in her niece's voice. "Roni, is there something I should know?"

Veronica turned away from the window. "No, Aunt Mel. Everything is fine." She walked away.

Melanie folded her arms and turned back to the window as Rafe's Mercedes pulled out of the driveway. He better not even think about "charming" her niece.

Traci had made herself quite at home in Claude's space, waiting on him hand and foot. She'd even told Lin that she could take the rest of the week off because she would be more than happy to look after Claude. She felt like the lady of the house and thought that it might be time to act on it.

She took extra time and care getting bathed and dressed. She wanted Claude to really see her, not as a former affair and now "the good friend" but as a woman who could make him happy. Claude wasn't the kind of man who needed some dating service to get a woman. He had her, if he would only look. When they'd met for dinner that night and he told her in so many words that he'd prefer a blind date than having a relationship with her, it tore her up inside. She'd tried to be cavalier about it, hiding her real feelings, but she couldn't. It had been killing her and she'd wanted to tell him how she really felt before it was too late, and then she got the call about the accident.

It was as if fate had finally dealt her a winning hand and given her the chance that she needed to make Claude hers.

She took a final look in the mirror, fixed a smear from her lipstick and walked out of her bedroom. Claude was downstairs. She could hear the music from the stereo. He was moving around much better and had said that the pain in his ribs was all but gone. All good signs. But time was not on her side. She didn't have weeks to wait. Her postponed trip to Turkey was rescheduled. She had to leave in two days. She wanted her position with Claude established and locked before she left, and she was certain that one night together would make him remember how good it was between them and could be again, for good.

She descended the stairs and walked up behind him. He was seated on the couch with his head back against the cushions. His eyes were closed. She leaned over and kissed him lightly on his forehead. His eyes opened. He sat up and turned to look at her over his shoulder. His dark eyes ran quickly over her body that was barely covered by a sheer floral robe that served as a flimsy coverup for her thong and nothing else.

She came around to sit beside him.

"Traci…"

She put her finger to his lips. "Shh, just listen."

But she didn't talk—she leaned closer and pressed her lips to his. Her tongue teased the fullness of his mouth, longing for access. She looped her arms around his neck while she pushed her hot body flush against him.

She felt so good against him. She smelled so sweet, her scent filling his head. He remembered how good it was between them and how he felt afterward. He clasped her arms and gently removed them from around his neck, breaking the kiss.

Traci sat back, her eyes still heated with longing. "What's wrong?" she managed to say. Her heart pounded. She stroked his cheek. He took her hand and put it down in her lap.

"Let's not do this, Traci. You know that I care about you. We had some great times together, but it can never be more than what it was and that's not fair to you and it's not fair to me."

She blinked rapidly as the reality of what he was saying began to resonate within her and tears threatened to overflow. "You have no idea how I feel about you."

"I do and that's why I'm telling you this. It can't work."

"Why—because I'm white?" Her question carried

the ring of a child who can't believe there is no Santa.

"No." He squeezed her hand. "You know me better than that. It's us, Traci. It takes more than great sex to make a relationship and that's what it's been between us," he said as gently as he possibly could. "It takes deep feelings and commitment. And I don't feel that way about you to make a long-term commitment. I never wanted to hurt you," he said, knowing how hollow and cliché it sounded.

She lowered her head, nodded slowly and wiped her eyes.

Claude lifted her chin with the tip of his finger and looked into her eyes. "You deserve someone to love you, Traci. And I know you'll find him or he will find you."

"This is awkward," she said, forcing a smile behind her tears and finding someplace to look other than into his telling eyes. Slowly she stood. "Thank you for being honest with me. I guess it hit me that I was on the verge of losing what we had when you told me about the service you were using. I wasn't ready to let go." She sniffed.

"I don't know what else to say other than I'm sorry."

She straightened her shoulders. "I'm a big girl. You don't have to apologize for being honest. I appreciate that."

He stood. He wanted to hug her and tell her that everything would be fine, but he didn't want that to lead to anything that couldn't be fulfilled.

"I'm going to leave in the morning, get ready for my trip."

He nodded.

"So I guess that's it then."

"Yeah," he murmured.

"I'll give you a call next time I'm in town…see how you're doing."

"I'd like that."

She pressed her lips together to keep them from trembling, turned and went back upstairs.

Claude flopped down onto the couch, wincing slightly. It was the right thing to do, he told himself. If there ever was a real chance for the two of them, it dissolved after the night he'd spent with Melanie. But it didn't appear that he would have her in his life either. What he needed was a fresh start—the start that TPS could provide for him. He'd find a woman who could totally erase memories of Traci and especially Melanie. They guaranteed satisfaction, and he was going to hold them to it.

"We have Mr. Lawson all set for his first date. I think he and Dominique will be perfect," Veronica said. "She can definitely stand her ground with him."

"Great. I'm eager to hear how they feel about each other."

"Any word from Mr. Montgomery?" Jessica asked.

Melanie swallowed. "No. I'm guessing he's still recovering from his injuries." *With the lovely Ms. Traci, no doubt.* "I'm sure he'll be in touch when he's up to it."

The office phone rang. Jessica answered. "Speak of the devil," she mouthed. "Of course, Mr. Montgomery. I'm sure I can get everything back on track. Both of the ladies are eager to meet you. Of course. Tomorrow afternoon would be perfect. Absolutely. See you then." She hung up the phone. "Mr. Montgomery will be here tomorrow afternoon to go over the tapes of our choices for him and decide on his first date."

Melanie's pulse was pounding so loud that she could barely make out what Jessica was saying.

"I'm going to go over all the details and make sure we didn't forget anything," Veronica said, getting up.

"And I have about five potentials to sort through that have been referred to us," Jessica said, following her cousin's lead.

Moments later, Melanie found herself alone. Claude would be there tomorrow. She could come up with a million reasons why she couldn't be there, but that would be childish. What happened between them happened. It was over, it was done, it was a mistake and it simply wouldn't happen again. She'd keep a low profile as she generally did when clients met with the team for consultation. She'd greet him when he arrived and wave goodbye when he left. Simple and utterly uncomplicated. And it was like Cynthia had concurred—she'd crossed the line and now she was going to have to deal with it.

He had to admit, though reluctantly, that the house seemed different now that Traci was gone. She definitely brought a certain energy with her. She seemed better, Claude thought as he dressed in preparation for his visit to TPS. They'd talked for a long while over coffee and bagels on the morning she'd left. What it all boiled down to was that she was getting older and scared. Her conversation with Claude about him finding someone to settle down with had rocked her more than she realized. It brought her life and how she lived it into sharp focus. She panicked, she'd said.

Claude pulled his slate-colored cotton knit shirt over his head, adjusting it along the lines of his body. He was glad they had talked before she left and cleared the air. He didn't want her to leave with hard feelings. There were too many years between them to throw it all away. She promised to stay in touch, if he promised to send her an invitation to his wedding whenever that may be.

He gazed into the mirror. The small stitch that he'd

received over his eyebrow as a result of the accident had healed nicely or as well as scars healed, he supposed.

He brushed the tip of his finger across the slight imperfection, getting acquainted with this new dimension of himself. He turned away from his reflection to put on his shoes, opting for loafers instead of ones that he would have to tie to avoid bending over. Although the pain in his ribs was almost gone, he still wasn't one hundred percent and he didn't want to do anything to aggravate the injury.

He grabbed a light jacket from the hall closet, put his wallet in the inside pocket, took his keys and let Lin know that he was leaving.

"No motorcycles!" she called out, bustling in from the kitchen.

Claude chuckled and assured her that there was no motorcycle in his immediate future. He was taking the Explorer and would probably be back late.

The day was brilliant. The air was exceptionally clear and still. There wasn't a cloud in the sky. The trees were in full bloom and their lush branches stood in sharp contrast against the blue sky.

Claude slowly inhaled the stillness of the air. He wanted to stretch and take it all in but, mindful of his ribs, he opted not to. He unlocked the SUV and got behind the wheel. While the engine warmed up, he checked his CDs and lined up a few to play on the road, plugged his cell phone into the hands-free outlet, then eased out of the driveway and onto the road.

Traffic was light as he proceeded onto the Hutchinson River Parkway, gliding along to the smooth sounds of Teddy Pendergrass. Hard to believe the world had lost so many legends in the past few years. Truly made you respect and appreciate each and every day, which was just another reason why he needed to seize the moment and plan for his future. Ever since Regina, he'd shut down a part of himself and operated on autopilot. He became his job. That was no way to live and nothing made it clearer than his night with Melanie. Maybe nothing could ever happen between them, but it wasn't all for nothing. He discovered that he still had the ability to feel, that sensation deep inside that made you warm, that made you smile, that made you want more. That's what Melanie had done for him and for that he would always be thankful.

By the time he'd reached the Cross Island Expressway, the late-morning rush-hour traffic had increased and, as usual, it was bumper-to-bumper to get on the Long Island Expressway heading out toward the Hamptons. It seemed that even midweek, folks planned for getaways and long weekends, although there were many New Yorkers who commuted.

As he drew closer to Sag Harbor Village, the

signage indicated ten miles, five, two, turn right, "Welcome."

His pulse kicked up a notch. Shortly he'd pull up to the TPS mansion. He was sure that Melanie would be there or perhaps it was wishful thinking. He did want to see her again, even in passing. He'd made up his mind that a relationship with her wasn't possible. She didn't want it, and he never went after a woman who didn't want him. He made a short left and followed the narrow cobblestone road through the center of the village, then out toward the house.

What if he told her how he really felt about that night or that he hadn't stopped thinking about her since the night they'd met. What if...

His cell phone rang. The lighted dial identified the caller as Senator Lawson.

"Sir. Good morning."

"Claude, how are you?"

"On the mend."

"Glad to hear it. Things are moving along. My plate is full and we need you back as soon as possible. Hastings is good as deputy chief of staff, but he's not you. He doesn't have...people skills."

Claude half smiled at the compliment. "I'll be back in D.C. on Monday."

"Great. At least I know that everything with the staff and the upcoming conferences will be taken care of the way I like it when you're back on board.

At least the office will run smoothly even if my household is shot to hell."

The mansion was up ahead. He steered the car along the incline's sand and gravel road. "What do you mean? Is everyone okay?"

"The girls are fine. As usual. Just that damned son of mine."

"What's old Rafe up to now?" He pulled into the driveway. He turned off the engine. He took the call off speaker and removed the phone from its cradle.

"Same shenanigans." He chuckled deep in his throat. "Got him set up with that fancy dating service. And before the boy even goes out on a first date he's talking about having eyes for the owner."

Claude opened the car door and stopped short. "Rafe is using a dating service?"

"Yes, you were talking to the owner that night at the Embassy. Melanie Harte. She runs that fancy place out at Sag Harbor. Her grandmother, God rest her soul, got me and Louisa together."

Claude slammed the door. His jaw clenched. The senator was going on about how great the service was, but Claude had stopped listening. Knowing Rafe Lawson, he was sure that Rafe had been attracted to Melanie and wouldn't be shy about letting his feelings be known. Did she wind up taking him to bed, too? His jaw was so tight that his temples began to throb. He looked up at the house and thought about getting back in the car and going home.

"Looking forward to seeing you up on the Hill next week."

He released the breath he'd been holding. "Yes, see you then," he said absently before disconnecting the call. For several moments he stood rooted to the spot. He slammed his fist against the side of his SUV, then walked up to the front door.

Chapter 10

"Hey, Mr. Montgomery," Vincent greeted him. "Good to see you." He shook Claude's hand as he ushered him inside. "How are you feeling? Melanie told us about your accident. She was pretty worried. We all were."

I bet she was. "Thanks. I'm feeling pretty good. No lasting effects."

"Good to hear. I'm pretty sure Veronica and Jess are in the conference room waiting for you. I'll let Aunt Mel know that you're here." He led him to the door of the conference room and handed him over to the ladies. Claude walked in all smiles, but his mind was on Melanie.

* * *

From her bedroom window she saw the black Explorer pull into the driveway. She watched Claude get out. She'd hoped to feel nothing when she saw him again. But that pang in the center of her chest was as strong today as all the times before. She turned away. Any minute she'd hear the knock on her door and one of her family members telling her that Claude was here. Would he ask for her, or wait to see if she showed up? She could always say that she was busy. But that was cowardly. Why did this one man have her so twisted into knots? She virtually screamed in her head and wished that she could throw something without the cavalry coming to see what was wrong.

She didn't have time to plan out any more scenarios. Vincent was knocking on her door, telling her that they were all waiting for her downstairs.

"I'll be right there."

She listened for his footsteps to drift away. She stood in front of the mirror and concluded that she had never looked better. She drew in a long breath of steely determination and went downstairs to meet her client.

Laughter journeyed out into the foyer and with a crooked finger beckoned her to join in. Jessica was telling the story of the three of them when they went on their first camping trip together as teens and all came back with poison ivy.

"We were a mess," Vincent was saying. "And my dad was beside himself."

"Yeah," Veronica agreed. "Dad may be a lot of things, but he's all thumbs when it comes to stuff like that. He gets all weird and crazy with a lot of whiney kids." She laughed at the memory.

"You all seem really close," Claude said in admiration. Having been an only child he never had the experience of sharing memories or growing up with anyone else. He always wondered what it would have been like to share secrets, fears and triumphs with a sibling.

"Good morning, everyone."

They all turned in the direction of Melanie, who stood in the doorway. She came inside and extended her hand to Claude, who rose to greet her. "It's great to see that you're doing better. How are you feeling?"

He closed his fingers around her slender hand and all the anger, animosity, doubt and jealousy that he'd allowed to build up inside him began to evaporate. "Much better since we last saw each other." His smile was genuine and she returned it.

"Good, I'm glad to hear that," she said on a breath, the heat of his touch shooting up her arm. "Are you up to meeting your date?" Reluctantly she slipped her hand from his, the memories of his touch clouding her thoughts.

"Ready as I'll ever be."

She nodded. "Jessica will bring you up to speed, answer any remaining questions and get everything set up. After your date is over, we'll ask that you come back and give us an update on how it went, what your impressions were and we'll take it from there."

"Fine."

"Well… I'll let you all get to it. Oh, and I hope that you'll be available for our annual holiday party. It's in three weeks. Be sure to get the information before you leave."

"I will and I'll certainly try to make it if I'm available."

"It's *the* party," Veronica said. "We always have our clients attend, along with a host of others. Aunt Mel knows how to throw a bash."

"Sounds like fun." His eyes crinkled at the corners.

"Hopefully I'll see you before you go, if not then next week." She offered a tight smile and walked out, her heart hammering louder than the click of her heels against the wood floors.

Claude barely focused on the discussion while Veronica told him all about his prospective date with Grace. The pictures of her and her video introduction could have been abstract art for all that he understood. His mind was on Melanie. Seeing her again only brought to the surface the emotions that he'd tried unsuccessfully to tamp down. Melanie, however, didn't appear to hold the same sentiments. Her handshake was warm but her greeting could have been for any client, not one that you'd slept with.

It was clear that anything materializing between them was simply wishful thinking. One night does not a relationship make. For all he knew it may have been part of the sales package. He drew in a breath and forced himself to focus on the presentation.

Melanie couldn't stay in the house a moment longer, not with Claude right downstairs and her not being able to say what was on her mind. His behavior didn't give her a hint as to what he was thinking. And for Melanie to believe that his thoughts centered on her as much as hers did on him was a waste of her time. She'd called Cynthia and they agreed to meet for a late lunch. She needed some air and some space.

On her way out, her good manners and upbringing stopped her from walking out. She steeled herself and walked into the meeting room.

"I'm going out for a while but I wanted to say goodbye before I left."

Claude stood and she crossed the room and shook his hand, careful to keep her expression un-readable.

"Enjoy your date. Grace is a wonderful woman

and I'm sure you will find that you have a lot in common on many levels. I'll tell you, as I tell all of our clients, be open-minded and let the evening flow."

"I'll be sure to keep that in mind."

She gave a short nod, then looked beyond him to the assemblage at the table. "If you need me for anything, you can reach me on my cell." She smiled and walked out.

She concentrated on her purposeful stride, putting power in each step to drown out the pounding and sadness in her heart. As she got behind the wheel of her Jag she thought once again what a fool she had been to act on her impulses. Now she was paying for it, and the worst part was that the payment would be Claude in the arms of someone else.

After the fifteen-minute drive into the center of town and a bit of maneuvering, she found a parking space and walked back toward CG Gallery. Moving along with the leisurely pace of the afternoon foot traffic she smiled as she noticed the "Sales" signs in shop windows and the "Big Discount" advertisements announcing the end-of-season bargains. *Already*, she mused.

The town of Sag Harbor, though modern in most respects, still carried an air of its rich past, from the cobblestone streets, the turn-of-the-century lamp-posts, to quaint shops and ice cream parlors. From the center of town one could walk to the docks where sailboats and yachts were now docked, replacing the mighty trade ships of days gone by.

She enjoyed her life here. It had a calming effect on her spirit. That realization brought her up short, causing a young woman to bump into her. After a quick apology Melanie resumed walking. She'd done exactly what she'd vowed not to do from the moment she took over: mix her business with pleasure. The main reason for being in Sag Harbor and not Manhattan or L.A. was because of its easy-going lifestyle and its distance from the pressure and the maddening crowds, temptation and frenzied pace. She'd brought all of that drama to her doorstep. Her home, this town, was her sanctuary, a place of respite. And she'd muddied that and potentially jeopardized a business that had survived for decades on the edicts of professionalism, honesty and ethics.

She paused for a moment in front of the gallery, caught her reflection in the plate-glass window and swore she saw the image of her grandmother hovering over her shoulder. She was not pleased. *I'll make it right, Grandma. I'll make you proud.* She pushed through the swinging door and stepped inside.

Cynthia was with a client, so Melanie took the time to look around and see what new pieces Cynthia may have added to the collection. Although Cynthia was a strong advocate for black art and artists, her tastes were eclectic and the collection reflected it, from the paintings of unknown and famous artists from Europe, India and Africa to sculpture, pottery and jewelry from local residents. The gallery was one of the centerpieces of Sag Harbor, drawing art enthusiasts to the novice from near and far.

Melanie was so proud of her friend, who'd financed her dream on a credit card and built it to what it was today, and she never missed an opportunity to point someone in Cynthia's direction. If you didn't love art before, you would after meeting Cynthia and visiting the gallery.

Her business in the past ten years had blossomed from a small storefront to a two-story loft space that could accommodate up to 300 guests for a showing. The recession had slowed things down dramatically but business had picked up once again, as evidenced by the number of people in the gallery in the middle of the day mid-week.

Melanie wandered over to the jewelry case to look at some of the new silver pieces that had been added from a jewelry maker in Nigeria.

"Well, well. This is truly my lucky day."

Melanie turned and came face to face with Raford Lawson.

Chapter 11

For a moment she was speechless. The last person she expected to see was Rafe Lawson. "Mr. Lawson, what are you doing here?" Her thoughts quickly jumped to conclusions but were just as quickly dispelled.

"Cynthia called me and told me that my piece had arrived and the framing was done. So here I am." He grinned, flashing his charm. "And you?"

Before she could answer, Cynthia joined them. "Sorry, about that Mel. Client took longer than I thought," she said, bussing her cheek with a quick kiss. She turned glowing eyes and pearly whites on Rafe. "Good to see you."

He took her hand and drew her in. He kissed her cheek. "Always good to see you and our mutual friend," he added, turning to Melanie.

"Melanie and I were about to head out to a late lunch. Why don't you join us?" she asked with an adoring gaze.

"I'd love to as long as I'm not imposing on girl talk time," he said addressing his statement toward Melanie.

"It's fine with me."

"It's settled then, and it's my treat since I am the third leg."

"You get no complaints from me," Cynthia said. "Let me get my purse and let Neal know that I'm leaving for the day. I'll meet you both out front. Oh, is B. Smith's okay with everyone?"

They both agreed.

"Good, I'll be right back. We can pick up your painting afterward, unless you want to load it into the car now."

"Sure, if it's not too much trouble I'll take it now."

"No problem." She darted into the back room and returned moments later with his art wrapped in brown paper and tied with string. "Here you are. I know it will look fabulous on any wall."

"I already have a place in mind. Right over the fireplace at the cabin in Vermont."

"Sounds lovely," Cynthia said and seemed genuinely rooted to the spot as she stared openly at Rafe.

Melanie cleared her throat and Cynthia's cobwebs.

She blinked. "Uh, I'll join you both in a sec." She hurried off again.

Rafe watched her walk away, then turned to Melanie. "I'm going to put this in the car."

Melanie tucked her purse under her arm and followed him out. He needed watching.

They stepped into the late afternoon. The sun had begun to grow lazy and was overcast with brewing storm clouds. It gave the town a Norman Rockwell feel.

"My car is right there." He pointed to a Mercedes three cars down. They walked together. Rafe popped the trunk with the remote and slid the painting inside.

"What did you buy?" Melanie asked as he shut the trunk in time to a distant drum of thunder. The wind kicked up and the skies grew dark.

Rafe reached out and brushed a flyaway strand of hair from her face. He explained to her about the piece of art he'd purchased as an SUV slowed beside them but didn't stop.

Thankfully he had been cruising down the street, taking in some sights as the vehicle in front of him loomed into view, Claude realized, or he would have surely rear-ended it. He pulled into a handicapped space toward the end of the street and watched the scene behind him unfold through his driver's side mirror.

She was looking up at him, laughing and nodding, and she had no problem with him touching her hair or her arm as he spoke. He ushered her to the passenger-side door, hurrying out of the sudden splatter of rain with his arm protectively around her waist. He helped her inside, then hurried around the front and got behind the wheel.

He'd seen enough, more than enough. He peeled away from the curb, startling everyone in range on the otherwise-quiet strip.

"Somebody's in a hurry," Rafe said, looking into his rearview mirror just as Cynthia darted to the car and got in.

"Wow, the weatherman needs a new job," she said, shaking off her umbrella.

They laughed.

"Which way copilot?" Rafe asked Melanie, putting the car in gear.

"At the corner make a left and I'll direct you from there."

By the time Claude reached the highway, the rain was falling at a steady pace. He kept replaying the scene over and over in his head. Every way he looked at it, nothing changed. Melanie had left the house to meet Rafe Lawson. He didn't want to let his mind take him to that dark place. He didn't want to think that way about her. But if nothing was going on, if there was nothing to hide, why not say that she was going to meet Lawson in front of everyone? What was there to hide?

The questions twisted and turned, churning in his head until he felt like it would explode.

Why did it matter he asked himself repeatedly on the long, lonely drive home. Why?

Chapter 12

The car would arrive shortly. Claude took his midnight-blue suit jacket from the closet and slipped it on. Maybe Grace Freeman would be the one, he thought, while he smoothed his pearl-gray shirt. Since he'd seen Melanie and Rafe, he'd worked extra hard to keep thoughts of her at bay. Hopefully a night out with a beautiful, intelligent and talented woman would wipe images of Melanie from his head altogether.

According to Jessica, the perfect evening was planned and he was determined to make the most of, give Grace his undivided attention and remain open to possibility.

He heard the front doorbell ring and then Lin's footsteps. Moments later she was tapping on his bedroom door.

"Mr. Montgomery, the driver is here. Oh, my, don't you look handsome," she beamed, taking in his tall, muscular figure in the Ermenegildo Zegna suit. She came around behind him and reached up to adjust the back collar of his jacket.

"Thank you, Lin."

She moved to stand in front of him. She looked up into his eyes. "I don't mean to pry, Mr. Montgomery, but for weeks now you haven't been yourself. You seem sad and distant, which is so unlike you." She lowered her gaze for a moment, then looked back at him. "I hope that this evening will bring your smile back."

Before he could respond she left the room and hurried downstairs. For a moment, Claude was completely stunned. Had his emotions been that obvious? He always prided himself on keeping his feelings hidden deep beneath the surface. He glanced at his image in the mirror. He was more determined than ever to make this evening work.

Seated in the plush interior of the limo, he smiled with pleasure. When Jessica reiterated that TPS was a classy organization she wasn't kidding. The limo was fully equipped and the driver was professional yet attentive. If this was any indication as to what the rest of the evening would be like, perhaps he was in for a treat.

Grace lived about forty minutes away in Parkchester. As they drew closer to her home, Claude actually grew nervous. Even though he'd seen her pictures, got the inside story of her life and accomplishments and watched her interview, it was still equivalent to a blind date. He hadn't been on one of those since a dare in college, and that turned out to be an awful experience. He rubbed his damp palms together. Just relax, he kept reminding himself—she's probably just as nervous as he was.

Shortly, the car slowed onto Grace's block, which was composed of modest single-family homes with long driveways and manicured lawns on a tree-lined street. From what he knew of Grace, this setting was what he would have expected. He smiled.

The driver parked at the curb and came out to open his door.

"Thank you. We should be right out."

"Take your time, sir. The drive is not that long."

Claude nodded. He slipped his suit jacket back on as he stepped out of the car. The air had cooled considerably as the days had already begun to grow shorter. Before long summer would come to an end and the rush of the holiday season would be upon them. He glanced up for a moment before walking down the path to the front door. The sky was clear.

The whites of the clouds looked like a portrait against the night sky. A sprinkling of stars beyond the half moon made the perfect picture. Maybe it was all a sign of good things to come. He stepped up to the front door and rang the bell. He could hear the soft chimes reverberate inside the house. Moments later, Grace opened the door with such a smile of welcome that she made you feel that you'd come home after a long time.

She extended both hands and covered his. "It is so good to meet you in person."

Grace Freeman was thinner than her video, with skin the color of golden sand, hazel eyes etched with long, dark lashes and thick, naturally wavy ink-black hair that framed her angular face and fell softly to her shoulders. Her name suited her. She had the regal bearing of royalty but without the pomp and circumstance.

"It's a pleasure to meet you face to face, as well."

She smiled even brighter. "Please come in. Do we have time?"

"The driver assured me that the ride is short."

"Great. Come on in. I'll give you the ten-cent tour." Her laughter sounded like music, and the tension that had tightened the center of his chest began to loosen.

He followed her inside and stepped down into the

foyer which was rich and cozy with color and flowers and books. Logs burned in the fireplace and the soft lighting gave the space an intimate feel.

"Did you have any trouble finding the house?" she asked.

"No not at all. You have a wonderful home."

"Thank you. If I could just decorate with books I would be very happy," she said. "It's my passion, as you can tell."

"I noticed. But I would be very concerned about a writer who *wasn't* in love with books."

She laughed. "You definitely have a point. Right through here is the dining room, small but functional." They walked through it, turned a small corner and came into the kitchen.

Where her living and dining rooms were traditional in feel, her kitchen was the complete opposite. It was ultra modern, totally high tech, all white with stainless steel appliances and accessories along with an island counter for cooking and a built-in wok and working sink. Her oven was restaurant size, accompanied by two matching microwaves and an array of blenders and steamers. Sparkling pots hung from ceiling racks, and a corner curio was lined with cookbooks and spices.

"I take it your other passion is cooking," he teased.

"Oh, can you tell?"

They laughed.

"Books and food. That's my world."

"I'm sure it's more than that."

She angled her head to the side and looked at him. "I suppose it is," she conceded as if processing the information for the very first time. "Can I get you something to drink?"

"No, thanks, I'm fine."

"Then I'll get my coat and we can go." She led him back to the front.

"I just have to run upstairs. I'll be right down."

"Take your time." He sat down on the couch and picked up one of her novels from the coffee table. *Horizons* by Grace Freeman. He turned it to the back and read the blurb. It was a novel about a small town in the West in the late 1800s totally populated by blacks. It was touted by *The New York Times, USA Today* and *The Washington Post* as a brilliant look at a little-known fact of American history. Right next to it was a paperback romance also bearing her name.

Claude flicked a brow in admiration. Her writing was as eclectic as her living space.

"Ready." She had her purse in her hand and her evening shawl draped over her arm.

He returned the book to the table and stood.

"Are you a romance reader?" she asked, with a sparkle in her eyes.

"Uh, can't say that I am." He chuckled.

"Most men would be surprised at how good they actually are."

"Hmm. What would my boys think if they saw me reading a...what do they call them...oh yeah, bodice rippers."

She laughed out loud. "They'd think it took a *real* man to read a romance."

"Yeah, after they stopped laughing."

"You're probably right."

He helped her adjust her shawl across her shoulders and then reached around her to open the door. He caught a whiff of her scent and with it a rush of memories. It was the same perfume that Melanie wore. It rocked him. Seeped down through his pores and streamed through his blood.

"Are you okay?"

He looked and Grace was staring at him. He blinked. Tried to push the soft, sensual scent away, but it came closer and touched his hand.

"Claude?"

"Oh." He shook his head and forced a smile. "Sorry. Thought I forgot something."

She frowned slightly. "Did you?"

"No. I didn't forget."

"Okay. Can you pull the door shut? It slam locks."

He did as asked and walked beside her to the car

and wondered how he would get through the rest of the evening.

In the close quarters of the car the scent of her perfume clouded his head. While they drove Grace talked about her career as an author, her travels and the fascinating people she'd met and, oddly enough, her shyness.

The gentle cadence of her voice untied the knots in his gut and helped to stem the tide of images of Melanie's body wrapped around his, her smile, electricity and the sensation of coming alive again.

They arrived at Madame X on Houston Street in Manhattan and walked through the rooms to where the "Lady Jane's Salon"—a live reading session with romance authors—was already under way. After giving their names, they were escorted to their table and a hostess took their orders while they listened to the erotic reading.

The atmosphere was charged with laughter and energy and Claude couldn't help but get caught up in it. This was definitely a first for him. The sultry décor, red velvet couches, draperies and lounge chairs gave the space an elegant decadence.

"So this is what you write?" he asked with a smile, getting comfortable on the couch where they'd been seated.

She nodded. "Not quite as steamy, but in the ballpark. And before you ask—no, none of my characters are me. I'm nowhere near as interesting."

The waitress arrived with their drinks and took their orders for appetizers. Jessica had set them up to have a late dinner at Karuma Zushi on the East Side. The renowned Japanese restaurant was known for flying in the fish from Japan along with special Japanese ingredients. People traveled from far and wide to sample the chef's omakase, which was one hundred dollars a plate.

Claude raised his glass. "To a wonderful evening."

Grace touched her glass to his. "To new friends."

They sipped their drinks. The hostess and one of the founding authors of Lady Jane's Salon, Leanna Renee Hieber, approached the mic.

"That was Gwynne Forster, everyone. Let's give her another round of applause." She waited until the applause died down. "Tonight we have a surprise guest to read for us. Even she will be surprised. Please join me in welcoming to the stage Ms. Grace Freeman!"

Grace's mouth opened but no words came out. Claude was just as stunned but, even more, he was amused. "Don't just sit there," he said as he leaned across the table. "Get on up there and wow the crowd."

"I'm totally unprepared," she said in a loud whisper.

"Come on and let me see you do your thing."

Grace took a deep breath and willed herself up from the seat. The applause grew until she reached the stage. Leanna was grinning as if she'd won something. She leaned close to Grace and kissed her cheek, then whispered in her ear. "Melanie asked me to do her this favor. I have your book on the stand by the mic."

Grace stood in front of the mic and looked into the packed room. She thanked everyone and explained how she wasn't prepared for this but she would find a section to read.

Claude leaned back and watched her, totally impressed with her skill and ease in front of a crowd. The portion she read from her romance was racy but not quite as over the top as the previous writer.

When she was done she returned to her seat to the sound of applause and foot stomping. She slid back into her seat next to Claude.

"You were fantastic," he said.

"Thanks." She shook her head in disbelief. "I can't believe that happened or that the Society would arrange for something like this."

"I kinda liked it. Almost made me want to go out and buy a romance novel."

She tossed her head back and laughed.

* * *

Dinner at Karuma Zushi was beyond explanation. They were waited on hand and foot. Every wish was anticipated. The food was incredible, and the service and the atmosphere were impeccable.

On the ride home they laughed and talked about their unconventional evening and how much they had enjoyed the two extremes. It was well after midnight when the limo pulled up in front of Grace's home.

The driver came around and opened the door. Grace and Claude got out and he walked her to the front door.

"I hope you enjoyed yourself tonight," Grace said as she stood framed in the doorway.

"I did," he said quietly then slid his hands into the pockets of his slacks.

"I'm going to be honest," she said.

He looked into her eyes.

"I think you're great. You have an exciting life. But I don't think we…you and I…are the connection we're looking for. At least not long term."

"Why…I thought—"

She held up her hand to stem the flow of his explanation. "Whoever she is, she's important to you," she said softly. "And it's okay." She touched his hand. "It's in your eyes. A woman knows these things."

"I don't know what to say…"

"Say you'll call from time to time or whenever you get things settled with her."

He leaned down and kissed her cheek. "You're fabulous," he said and meant it. "And I think I'm going to pick up your romance novel."

She tossed her head back and laughed and wagged a finger at him. "A good romance is just the medicine you need."

He took her hands. "Thank you, Grace, for tonight, for understanding, for sending me on my way."

"I'm happy that we had the chance to meet. Perhaps at another time in each of our lives things would have been different." She shrugged lightly.

He nodded. "Good night, Grace."

"Good night."

He turned and went down the stairs.

"Don't forget to post your review on Amazon," she called out. That warm laughter in her voice followed him down the steps.

He glanced over his shoulder. "I will."

On the ride back home in the limo, Claude went over the night in his head. He was sure that he'd been attentive and acted like a gentleman and he'd truly enjoyed the evening. Grace was a wonderful woman. What had been the tip-off to her that his mind and heart were elsewhere? Even Lin made reference that he hadn't been himself.

As he prepared for bed he knew that part of what

was holding him back not only from Grace but from living life to its fullest was a freak accident. Right up to today he still remembered getting the call, not understanding what was taking Regina so long to get to the church. The guests were getting restless. So it made no sense to him what the officer on the phone was saying. Accident. Truck. Regina. Fatal. Sorry.

He crawled under the covers. The sheets were cool against his skin. He buried his feelings when he buried Regina. That was how he was able to survive, to move from one day to the next. Until he grew weary of the emptiness.

He turned out the bedside lamp and rolled onto his left side. He'd hoped that when he found someone it would be gradual, building from an attraction, to friendship, to love. That was the way it had happened with him and Regina. He never expected Melanie. She went against the way he'd planned it in his head and he couldn't deal with that. Not to mention that she, in essence, worked for him.

How twisted was that? Not to mention that no matter what he may be feeling or thinking, it was all business to Melanie.

He closed his eyes and willed himself to sleep. Was she with Rafe right now?

Chapter 13

Melanie barely slept a wink. Throughout the night her dreams were plagued with images of Claude and Grace. Her business side hoped that the evening was wonderful for the both of them. But Melanie the woman hoped that it was a flop.

She couldn't remember ever being in such an awful position. This was so unlike her not to have total clarity in her life. She always knew what she wanted and how she was going to get it, but from the moment she'd met Claude, all things rational went out the window and it was making her crazy. This was the kind of thing that happened in novels and chick flicks, not to her.

To compound the problem her sense of judgment had gone out the window, as well. She'd been wrong about everything lately, particularly about Rafe Lawson and Claude Montgomery. Neither of them had been what she'd expected and had shot her theories about them straight to hell. What did that say about her ability to do her job, to find the right matches, if she could be so utterly wrong in her own life?

Maybe what she needed was to get away for a little while and gain some perspective. But with the planning of the party in full swing, now wasn't the time. Somehow she'd have to work her way through it.

At least the house was quiet today. Jessica was at her apartment in town. Veronica had a date, Vincent and Cherise were away for the weekend and Evan was off until Monday. Melanie was in the big sprawling house alone.

She wandered downstairs and went to retrieve the paper from the front steps, then went to the kitchen to fix a pot of coffee. While the coffee perked she flipped through the paper, stopping to read the headlines.

She poured her coffee and sipped thoughtfully. Today was a new day, she determined. What was done was done. It was time to move on. She snapped the paper closed and took her coffee to her office. Just as she sat down at her desk, the business line rang. She started to let it go to voicemail but decided to answer just before the message came on.

"Hello?"

There was a moment of hesitation. "Hello. This is Claude Montgomery."

Her heart thumped. "Good morning," she said, pushing cheer and enthusiasm into her voice.

"Sorry to call on the weekend, but I'll be leaving to go back to D.C. Sunday night. I, uh, know that Veronica was anxious to hear what happened last night."

"Oh." *Going back to D.C.* "Everyone is off today. I'm actually here alone. How did it go?"

"Everything that you all did was wonderful. No complaints. Grace is…a fabulous woman."

She could hear the "but" coming and almost welcomed it.

"We both decided that…well she decided that it wasn't going to work."

There was an immediate sense of relief, almost exultation, which she hid behind a barrage of words. "Sometimes even our best efforts don't always work the first time. I know that Veronica will want to speak with you more in-depth about what we could have done better," she rambled on until he cut her off.

"It wasn't anything that The Society did or didn't do. I don't want you to think that at all. It's…it's me. I thought this was something that I wanted but maybe I'm not as ready for commitment as much as I thought I was."

Her shoulders slumped. Whatever faint inkling of hope she'd harbored was dissolving with every beat of her heart. "I see."

"So, I want to thank you for everything. For trying. I don't see what sense it makes to drag this out and put Dayna through this with probably the same outcome."

"You don't know that," she said, suddenly desperate—not to hold onto a client but to not let Claude go. Even if he was with another woman, she still, in some weird way, had him in her life. "Why don't we...talk about this some more before you make a final decision?"

"Like I said, I'm leaving on Sunday and I need to start packing."

"I could come to you," she blurted out. "I mean, we could meet, in Manhattan."

"Is holding onto a client that important to you?" he asked, his tone suddenly sharp and accusatory.

"What?"

"Look, you can keep the fifty grand if that's what you're concerned with."

Her neck snapped back. "We don't need your money, Mr. Montgomery. Our business is built on satisfied clients. And the list is long."

"I'm sure it is," he said, the sarcasm sharp and hurtful. "Do you make sure that all of your clients get the same treatment that I did?" There, he'd said it, the question that had tormented him from the moment he'd opened his eyes and found the space in the bed next to him empty.

Melanie was so stunned she couldn't speak.

Hot, tension-laced air hung between them.

"I'll have the check delivered by messenger," she said, finding her voice, though she barely recognized it. "Do what you want with it. Have a good day, Mr. Montgomery." Her hand shook as she hung up the phone.

Is that what he thought of her? Oh God. Her eyes burned with tears of shame. She had no one to blame but herself. She looked at the phone. She was so tempted to pick it up and call him back. Explain that night. Explain why she'd left. Explain how she'd been feeling ever since. She reached for the phone and before she could talk herself out of it, she hit "last call" and his number dialed.

Her pulse raced as she listened to the ringing, waiting what seemed to be an eternity before it was answered.

"Montgomery residence."

Was this the woman from the hospital? Her brain seemed to freeze and she couldn't think.

"Hello? Montgomery residence," the voice repeated.

Melanie cleared her throat. "Yes, I was calling for Mr. Montgomery."

"I'm sorry. You just missed him. May I take a message?"

"Oh…no, thank you."

"May I tell him who called?"

"Don't worry about it. I'll try him later. Thank you." She hung up before she was pressed for any more details.

She covered her face with her hands. Her insides shook. Was he really gone? Did he know it was her and simply refused to answer? Who was that woman?

The questions ran behind each other like children playing follow the leader.

She pushed back from her seat and stood, then began pacing the room. Maybe it was best that he didn't answer after all. She probably would have only made matters worse. If that were possible. She inhaled deeply. There was nothing she could do about it now. She returned to her desk and pulled out the checkbook from the drawer.

In the history of the company they'd never returned a client's money. As she filled in the amount of fifty thousand dollars, she consoled herself with the fact that there was a first time for everything. Her next hurdle would have to be explaining it to the team. At least she had a couple of days to think about what she would say. Just before she stuck the check in an envelope she ripped it into tiny pieces and threw it away. She took out her personal checkbook and rewrote the check from her account. Simply because she'd been a fool was no reason for the business to pay the cost of her stupidity.

After she wrote the check she called the messenger service that she used. She wanted the check off of her desk, out of her house and in his hands sooner rather than later. The service assured her that someone would be there within the hour.

With that nasty task out of the way, she went downstairs to the home gym in the hopes of working off some of her frustrations.

As promised, the messenger service arrived and she handed over the check. The sun was still high in the sky. A balmy breeze blew in from off the water. She could hear the laughter of beachgoers in the distance. She shut the door behind her. A perfect day. And she had no one to share it with.

Just as she was heading upstairs to look for a good book to curl up with, she heard the sound of a car pulling into her driveway. Must be one of the kids, she thought until she heard the doorbell ring.

She went back down and came face to face with the last person she expected to see.

"What are you doing here?"

"Is that any way to greet your clients?" His grin was infectious.

"Come in, Mr. Lawson."

"I thought we'd gotten past that," he said, stepping inside.

"Rafe." She smiled and shook her head. "You still haven't answered my question."

"Actually, I finally took the painting out of my trunk and opened it up. Don't know if all the banging around did it, but the frame was cracked. I just took it back to the gallery to have it fixed. Cynthia was off today." He shrugged and his dimple winked at her. "I was in the neighborhood."

"Hmm, ummm. You should be home getting ready for your date tonight."

"Oh, I figure I'll just throw something on." He chuckled.

"Yeah, right. Can I get you something to drink?"

"Sure." He shoved his hands into his pants pockets. "Getting a little muggy out there. But at least you get the breeze from the ocean."

"Thankfully. Come on in the kitchen."

He followed her out. "House is quiet."

"Yeah, everyone is off today. Have a seat. Tea, coffee, juice?"

"Whatever you're having." He took off his jacket and hung it on the back of the chair and sat down.

She poured him a mug of coffee, then took the half and half from the fridge and brought both to the table. She sat opposite him. "I think you'll really enjoy your evening tonight."

"I'm sure I will." He lightened his coffee just a bit and dropped in a cube of sugar.

"Why do you do this?" he asked, looking at her over the rim of his mug.

"Do what?"

"Spend all your time getting other people together?"

"I enjoy making people happy."

"What about you?"

"What about me?"

"Who makes you happy?"

She glanced away. "No one at the moment. This isn't—"

"Maybe I could," he said cutting her off.

She drew in a sharp breath. She looked him square in the eye and was stunned to see what almost looked like sincerity in his brandy-toned eyes. "I don't get involved with my clients." *At least not anymore.*

"We can fix that right up." He reached into the pocket of his jacket and pulled out his checkbook. "Fifty grand, right?"

"What are you doing?"

"Giving you back your money. If I'm not a client, you don't have any excuse not to take me up on my offer of making you happy."

Had the whole world gone crazy in one day or was it just her? What was going on?

"Don't be silly. I'm not going to take your money. And I'm not going to get involved with you." She stood and folded her arms.

Rafe chuckled and slowly stood up. He looked down into her upturned face. "I always get what I want, cher, and I don't have to pay for it. It may take some time, but I do. So get ready." He took his coat from the chair. "Thanks for the coffee. I'll be sure to let you know how the date went." He turned and walked out.

Moments later she heard the front door close and the sound of Rafe's car engine. She stood there until she couldn't hear anything except the pounding of her heart.

Chapter 14

Claude returned home from his doctor's appointment with an all-clear to return to work. Getting back into the swing of the job was just the medicine he needed. The past month and a half had been a pure roller coaster ride: from meeting Melanie, sleeping with her, the accident, the mess with Traci and now today's blowup with Melanie. He'd come full circle, and he wanted to get as far away from the center of the storm as possible.

He shook off his lightweight jacket, which he really hadn't needed, and hung it on the hook in the hallway. The house was quiet. Lin must have left early to beat the thunderstorm that had been building all day.

He walked into the living room and turned on the television. The weatherman was trying to explain the unexpected storm that was powering across the East Coast. The weatherman needed a new job, he thought absently. He crossed to the bar and fixed a short drink. That's when he noticed the package on the table. He bent to pick it up. It was from a private messenger service. The address was from Sag Harbor. He ripped the envelope open. A small white envelope was inside. He opened it and took out the check. His jaw clenched. He stared at the neat handwriting before carefully folding it and tucking it in his back pocket. He fixed himself a drink, then went up to his bedroom to finish packing.

During the course of the next two weeks, Rafe had been set up on three perfect dates. Any one of the women would be right for him. They all but gushed when they spoke about the fabulous time they had, how attentive he was, how funny, sexy, such a gentleman. They couldn't wait to see him again.

Rafe, however, was lukewarm about each and every one, and it was driving Veronica crazy.

"I think he's intentionally giving us a hard time. This is a game to him," she said in frustration as she looked over a slide show of potential candidates.

"The thing that kills me," Jessica added, "is that he comes across as totally into them. If you listen to the women talk about the time they spent with him, you'd have no doubt that we'd done our job."

"Exactly. Until we talk to Rafe." Veronica shook her head.

Melanie listened without comment. It was a game to him. He'd said as much that night weeks ago at the Embassy. It was a challenge, something for him to do. She hadn't told Veronica or Jessica that he'd been to the house or what he'd said. It was probably all part of his game.

"For the time being let's not subject any more women to Mr. Lawson's endless charms," Melanie said. "We'll restrategize after the party. The next few days are going to be crazy and I don't want us to be distracted with Rafe's foolishness."

"And what's the story with Claude Montgomery?" Jessica asked. "I would have thought that he and Grace would have really hit it off."

Melanie ran her teeth across her bottom lip. "He had a change of heart." She shrugged. "It happens."

"But we promised Dad," Veronica said. "Maybe we should try again. I know there are—"

"Forget it!"

Two pairs of eyes landed on Melanie.

"Just forget it," she said with more calm.

"What's wrong, Aunt Mel?" Veronica asked. "You've been out of it for a while now. What's going on?"

"Nothing. I'm trying to focus on this party,

that's all. I have a lot on my mind. And if we have troublesome clients that we can't seem to satisfy, I say the hell with them." She pushed back from the table and stood, then walked out of the room, leaving her nieces with their eyes wide and their mouths open.

Melanie closed the door to her bedroom. She hadn't heard a word from Claude since she'd returned his money. She hadn't told the team that she'd even given it back. That would lead to questions of why and she wasn't ready to answer them. But she had heard from Rafe. Often. When he would call, the conversation would start off as business, generally a follow-up to a date and before long he would have her engaged in conversation about a movie that she must see, or a book he'd read, places they'd both traveled, music, politics, religion. Rafe Lawson was well-versed on many subjects, which is why she could see how the women he dated were totally captivated by him—in addition to which, he made you feel that listening to you was the most important thing he could do.

When she talked to him she had to keep her wits about her and not be sucked in by his southern charm, and, she had to admit, it wasn't always easy, especially if the call came late in the evening and she'd been thinking about Claude, who she'd catch glimpses of on the news from time to time among the cadre of politicos flanking the senator.

But it was getting a little easier. The sting wasn't as bad and she didn't beat herself up as regularly as she once did. Good signs, she consoled herself.

But today, for some reason, she'd lost it. She'd blown up at her nieces for no good reason, at least not one that she could explain to them, which was the fact that the party was in two days. They'd have a house full of guests. And she had no idea if Claude would be among them.

On the morning of the party the house was buzzing with activity and delivery trunks were in a waiting line to get to the front door. Party planners were busy in all of the rooms, draping, moving furniture, adding centerpieces and floral arrangements among other things. Coat racks were delivered and new linen had arrived for the tables along with extra tables, chairs, dinnerware and glasses. The catering trucks were unloading most of the morning and were finally setting up to begin preparing the food. The wait staff arrived at noon and were met by the head chef and the six bartenders. Vincent met with the head valet and attendant and gave instructions on where the cars should be parked. Spotlights had been set up on the lawn. A professional cleaning crew had been brought in to clean the house from roof to basement and would return for the big cleanup the morning after the party.

The guest list had been rounded out to one hundred

and fifty and all of them planned on attending. It was going to be a big, loud night. The two bands were scheduled to arrive soon so that they could set up and do sound checks.

Once all the players were in place, Melanie and the girls slipped out and let the party coordinator deal with all the details while they went to get their hair, nails and toes done.

"Ahhh," Veronica moaned in pleasure as hot sudsy water swirled around her submerged feet. She wiggled her toes.

"We've been doing this for years," Jessica said as she held her hand out to the manicurist. "You would think we'd be used to the craziness by now."

"I know, but it never seems to get easier. There are a zillion details even with a coordinator."

"Hey, Aunt Mel." Veronica peeked her head around her cousin. Melanie was seated in the next chair with her head back and her eyes closed.

"Hmm?"

"I was just thinking that with all this technology at our fingertips, we should move into the twenty-first century and have a virtual party."

Melanie opened her eyes and peered at her niece. "What?"

"You know, everyone could party from the comfort of their Web cam." She laughed at the novelty of the idea. "It would sure cut down on the craziness."

Melanie slowly shook her head. "That's what's wrong with you young people now. You've lost the art of conversation and socializing in the real world. Everyone is connected by a gadget, an email address or some social network that really only exists in cyberspace, wherever that is. The art of really getting to know people is being lost. I can pretend to be anyone I want behind a screen or some name I make up for my email address," she snapped, her tone growing testy. "But at some point you have to come out from behind all the façades and actually meet people face to face, write a real letter, without texting and deal with a person."

Her nieces looked at her for a moment, then they both laughed. "Aunt Mel, you are too funny. You're getting old."

She grumbled deep in her throat, then returned to her mini nap while her feet were being massaged. Of course technology had its place, she thought, drifting along on a cloud of relaxation. But it couldn't take the place of real communication. Sitting behind some computer screen, the person on the other end can't see your sincerity and you can't see theirs. They can't tell if you are lying, hurt, crying or even paying them any attention. You can be whoever you chose to be for the moment.

Just as she hid behind her screen and read Claude's

email that he'd sent to her personal BlackBerry early that morning.

Sry. won't b abl 2 attend. njoy ur party. sry 2 miss it. Regards 2 all. CM.

And that was it. He couldn't see the hurt in her eyes and she didn't have to pretend that it wasn't there.

By the time they returned to the house the decorators had turned the mansion into a virtual wonderland of lighting, drapery that hung from the ceiling encrusted with tiny crystals that made it shimmer and, incredibly, an ice sculpture in the center of the entryway. Beyond was the magnificence of the ocean, captured in the glow of the setting sun. The lights from the votives that had been placed throughout the space gave the entire atmosphere an elegant feel.

Mouthwatering aromas floated from the kitchen and the long linen-topped tables were ready for the platters of food that would fill them shortly. It was enough to take one's breath away.

The staff who had been hired for the festivities had all changed into their uniforms and were hurrying about to ensure that everything was taken care of.

The guests were scheduled to arrive in about two hours. The ladies went to their rooms to start getting ready. Melanie firmly believed that the hostess must be ready to greet the very first guest no matter how early they arrived. It was a credo that her grandmother had instilled in her, so she kept her eye on the clock as she bathed and dressed.

Although her preference was the short cocktail dress, for tonight's occasion she'd chosen a floor-length deep chocolate brown Vera Wang dress, strapless with a fitted bodice, jeweled across the top, fitted at the waist and tapered down to the hem just above her feet. A simple diamond necklace and matching earrings were her accessories. She wore her short hair cut away from her face, accenting her features with minimal makeup, which illuminated her near flawless complexion. Her sling-backed shoes were a perfect match for her dress. She added her favorite scent behind her ears and at her delicate wrists.

Within an hour she was ready and went to do a final check of every detail with the coordinator. Nothing was left to chance.

At precisely 7:00 p.m. the first guests began to arrive and the party started in earnest. Each time the bell rang, Melanie's stomach jumped. Even though Claude clearly said that he wouldn't be attending, she kept hoping that he would change his mind. Rafe was certainly in the house and charming every woman who came within proximity. It was quite amazing to watch. Several of the women he'd dated through the service were also in attendance and vying for his attention in one way or the other. It was like watching a real-life version of *The Bachelor*.

Melanie moved among her guests, hugging and kissing cheeks, dropping a bit of news here, picking up gossip there. From what she could tell everyone was having a great time and the staff didn't miss a beat. Not a glass was empty, not a dish out of place. The band knew when to pick up the beat and when to slow it down. The caterers kept the food coming and the bar was busy. However, she was very clear with the valets. No one was to get behind the wheel of a car if they even appeared to have had one drink too many.

Cynthia, who always stood in as a co-hostess, was totally engaged in conversation with a couple who'd met through The Society and were interested in buying art for the house they'd purchased after their wedding a year earlier.

They were moving into the third hour of the night when Veronica came up to Melanie. "Aunt Mel, have you heard from Dad? I thought he would have been here by now."

Melanie checked her watch. She frowned. "I thought so, too. He said he might be late but I didn't think he meant this late. Has he called?"

Veronica shook her head.

"I'll see if I can reach him." She hurried off to her office and closed the door. She went to her desk and dialed her brother's cell phone. It rang and rang until it went to voicemail. She left a message and hung up. A sense of unease moved through her, taking up residence in the center of her chest. She jumped at the sound of the ringing phone. It was her private line. It must be Alan calling to explain himself.

She snatched up the phone. "Where are you?"

"Melanie? It's me, Claude."

The heat of fear ran through her. It was in his voice. She gripped the phone. "Claude, I…I thought it was Alan calling me back. I'm sorry. He's late as usual. And I'm going to tell him about himself when he gets here. Everyone has been asking for him." Her thighs were trembling, but she knew she had to keep talking to keep Claude from saying whatever it was he called to say.

"Melanie. I'm sorry to be the one to call you. But I didn't want it to be anyone else."

She slid down into the chair because the air had stopped moving in and out of her lungs. She couldn't breathe. "What is it?"

"Alan had a heart attack. He was driving when it happened. He was flown to Georgetown University Hospital. I'm sending a car for you to bring you to the airport. It should be there in twenty minutes." He paused. "It's serious."

"Oh God, oh God." Not her brother. Not Alan. She couldn't think.

"Listen to me. When you hang up, go and tell the kids. Pack a bag and be sure you have ID."

Tears were streaming down her face.

"Mel. Are you listening to me?"

"Y-es."

"Good. I'll be here when you arrive. Someone from the State Department will meet you when you land in Washington."

She sniffed. "Okay." Mechanically she hung up the phone. For several seconds she stood there trying to process the information and then suddenly sprung into action. Her brother needed her. Now.

She wiped her face and went back out to the party. She searched for Cynthia and excused her from her guests. Quickly she told her what had happened and that she needed to leave immediately.

Cynthia squeezed her tight. She knew how close Melanie and Alan were and how much Mel adored her brother. "Don't worry about anything here. I'll take care of it."

"Thank you." She pressed her lips tightly together to keep from crying. "I have to tell the kids."

"I'll go with you."

They found Veronica, Vincent and Jessica in different parts of the house and broke the news as quickly and quietly as possible. Within moments they had their bags and were at the door when the SUV from the State Department pulled up to the front door.

Just as Melanie was making her exit, Rafe stopped her. "What's wrong? I'd know those suits anywhere," he said, indicating the government employees.

"Alan is in the hospital. He had a heart attack. It's serious." She tried to keep it together, but she felt as if she was going to break into a million pieces if she didn't see her brother and know that he was going to be all right.

"Oh, no. I'm sorry. Is there anything that I can do? Anything?"

"Help Cynthia out, give my apologies to the guests…"

"Of course." He squeezed her shoulder. "He's going to be okay. Alan is a tough guy. He'll come through this."

"I have to believe that." She turned and ran toward the waiting car.

Chapter 15

He didn't want to tell her how bad it really was, the fact that they'd almost lost Alan, not once but twice. The last code blue was barely an hour earlier. Every time he saw a doctor rush by his pulsed raced.

He felt so helpless. He wanted to do something. And if he drank another cup of coffee he was going to leap through the ceiling. He got up from the hard plastic chair and resumed his pacing. He checked his watch. It had been almost two hours since he had made the call. He'd gotten a text message from the agent assigned to get them to the airport that they'd boarded the plane and were en route. The flight was about an hour and a half. Hopefully they should arrive around one in the morning. He just hoped it wasn't too late.

* * *

The call. The drive. The flight. Melanie's head was pounding. She kept replaying Claude's words in her head, the severity with which they were delivered. And they were about her brother. She couldn't lose him. Not Alan. Each and every person that she'd ever loved she'd lost. Her grandmother, her mother, her husband Steven. Not Alan. She pressed her fist to her mouth so that she wouldn't scream. She didn't even realize how tightly she'd been gripping her nephew's hand until he patted her palm.

"It's going to be okay, Aunt Mel," he assured her.

She looked into his eyes and saw his father. Her throat clenched. She reached out and stroked his cheek. "I know, sweetheart." She prayed that they were both right.

By the time they reached the hospital and were ushered up to the cardiac critical care unit Melanie was shaking all over.

Claude jumped up from his seat and came to meet them as they came down the corridor.

When they saw each other, whatever may or may not have gone on between them no longer mattered.

Claude opened his arms and she walked right into them. He held her against him and for a moment kept the world and the reason why they were there at bay.

They blocked out the sounds of machines and fears and held each other.

He stepped back and looked down into her eyes. "He's going to be all right. He's strong."

She nodded, too afraid to speak.

Claude looked into the terrified faces of Alan's family.

"What happened?" Vincent asked.

Claude explained what he knew and brought them up to date on what the doctors told him so far. "The doctor is in there now," Claude concluded. "He's in the room down the hall." He put his arm protectively around Melanie's shoulder and led them down the hall, with Vincent holding the hand of his sister and cousin.

They stopped in front of a glass window. On the other side of the glass, Alan was connected to a series of machines and tubes. His chest barely rose and fell beneath the white sheet.

Veronica inhaled a sharp breath that sounded like bad brakes. "Dad," she whimpered.

A nurse was checking the tubes and writing notes on a chart. She turned to speak to the doctor. The doctor came out and met the family in the corridor.

"Doctor Fleming, this is Mr. Harte's sister, his son and daughter and his niece."

The doctor nodded to each of them in turn. "Why

don't we talk over here." He walked them down the hall to a small lounge. "Please sit."

Dr. Fleming held the chart in front of him as he spoke as if it could somehow protect him from any onslaught of emotion.

"Mr. Harte suffered a severe heart attack. Because it happened while he was driving and time was lost getting him out of the car…the EMS originally thought it was a typical accident and that he'd been knocked out when he ran into the divider…"

Melanie's stomach was swirling. Twisted images of her brother in his car flashed before her. He was on his way to the party, the party that she insisted he attend.

"…the delay in treatment caused a shortage of oxygen. He has had two more minor attacks since he's been here. Right now we're not sure if there has been damage to the brain. We won't know for sure until he wakes up."

"Wakes up?" Jessica cried.

"He's in a coma."

"Oh no."

The doctor held up his hand. "It's a good thing. It's giving his brain a chance to rest and heal," he said, trying to ease their anxiety.

"So you're saying that my brother is in a coma?" Her voice cracked in disbelief.

Claude tightened his hold on her hand.

"Yes."

"For how long?" Vincent asked.

"Hopefully no more than one or two days." He inhaled deeply. "I'll be back in the morning to check on him. You all are welcome to stay for a few minutes. One at a time. But then I'll have to ask that you leave. He needs all the rest he can get and you all do as well if you're going to help him recover." He nodded goodbye and walked away.

"Why don't you go in and sit with him a while, Melanie?" Claude suggested.

"Yes, go first, Aunt Mel."

Her throat worked but no words came out. Steeling herself she pushed through the glass door. For a moment she simply stood there, too stunned, too sad to move. The nurse waved her over.

"It's okay. Come and sit. Just be careful of the wires." The nurse stepped away from the bed.

Melanie stepped closer and gripped the guardrail on the bed. The beeping sound of the machine drowned out the pounding pulse in her ears. He looked like he'd aged five years. Her heart ached. She could never remember her brother being sick or weak or vulnerable. When they lost their dad before they got out of junior high, Alan had become the man of the house, looking after her, their sister and their mother. They were all gone. It was just the two of them against the world. They had to be there for Vincent, Victoria and Jess.

"We're going to get you through this, Al." She brushed her hand across his forehead and fought back the overwhelming desire to cry. "I love you, big bro. I'll be back tomorrow."

While Vincent, Victoria and Jessica took turns going to see Alan, Claude and Melanie stole a few minutes to talk.

"I can't thank you enough for arranging all this," she said to Claude as they sat side by side in the lounge.

"I knew none of you would be thinking clearly and would want to get here as soon as possible. Arranging things and people is what I do all day," he said with a soft smile.

Melanie looked into his eyes and for a moment felt safe and protected.

"It's going to be okay," he said softly. "You keep believing that."

She nodded.

"I know you didn't have time to think about where you were going to stay. My house in Dupont Circle is big, three floors, five bedrooms, plenty of space and you all are welcome to stay as long as you need to."

"Claude, no, we couldn't impose on you like that. An entire family descending on you..." She shook her head. "We'll stay at a hotel. There probably isn't a hotel in D.C. that I haven't stayed in at some point."

"You can try but there are two conventions going on. Hotels in the area are full. At least stay at my house for the night and you can try in the morning. Get some rest. It's late."

She was exhausted and she didn't have the energy to haggle with hotel clerks. "Okay, but just for tonight. Thank you."

"Don't worry about it. Come on."

Everyone was too drained and still in shock to put up too much of a fuss and before long they were settled in their rooms for the night.

But for Melanie, sleep wouldn't come. Her mind wouldn't slow down. She tiptoed out of bed with the intention of fixing some tea. She was glad her room was on the ground floor. She wouldn't have to worry about creeping down the stairs and possibly waking anyone up.

She eased her door open and walked down the hall to the kitchen. After a bit of looking around she found a box of tea and put some water on to boil. She sat at the table to wait. She rested her face in her hands and said a prayer for her brother, for her family.

"I thought I heard someone."

Her head jerked up. "I'm sorry. I didn't mean to wake you."

"You didn't. I couldn't sleep."

"Tea?"

"Sure." He pulled up a chair. "How are you holding up?"

"I don't even know, to tell you the truth." She smiled sadly.

He covered her hand with his. "We never talked… me and you."

The teapot whistled. She got up and went to the stove. "I know," she said with her back to him.

He came to stand beside her. He opened the cabinet above the sink and took out two mugs and set them on the counter. She took two teabags out of the box and put one in each mug. He poured the hot water.

"Honey or sugar?"

"Honey."

He took the honey from the cabinet and brought it to the table.

For several moments they sat in silence, sipping tea, thinking, needing to say things but unsure of how to begin or even if the time was right.

Melanie couldn't hold it in any longer. "There's… I've wanted to talk to you. Tell you…"

"Tell me what?" His eyes searched her face.

Then suddenly the words that had lived inside her for weeks she couldn't find. She couldn't say them.

"Then I'll tell you." He paused a moment. "From the moment I met you, you've been all I can think about, even when I don't want to. When we made love that night, it was more than some one night stand. I didn't want it to be. I wanted to tell you that, but you were gone. And when I did see you, you acted as if nothing happened." He shook his head as the vision of her and Rafe ran through his head. "I started thinking all kinds of things." He told her what really happened on his date with Grace, all about Traci and the loss of Regina. He was confessing his soul, making room for something, something better.

Melanie listened, at moments tickled, heartbroken, elated taking the emotional journey with him. When he finished he looked into her eyes. "No one would be right for me. No one except you. And that reality is so crazy sometimes that it doesn't make sense."

"Who can make sense of why they feel the way they do in a situation that defies explanation? I should have come to you. But I didn't. I went against everything that our business stood for. I crossed the line. I let my emotions lead me." She wrapped her hands around the mug. "So I had to stay away from you. And I thought it was the way you wanted it."

"It was never what I wanted. Never. I know this is not the time to hash out our issues, but I don't want the talking to stop here. The next few days and weeks are going to be hard on you and your family, on all of us. But I want you to be clear that no matter what, I'll be there for you, day or night."

A single tear fell from her eye and she quickly

wiped it away. Her throat was so tight and achy that her one word, "thanks," came out cracked and broken.

"Finish your tea. You need your rest. Tomorrow is going to be a long day."

The next three days were like living through a nightmare. The family took turns visiting with Alan, talking to him, praying for him. The doctors said that his vital signs were good. He was off the respirator and breathing on his own. All good signs, except that he had not awakened and the longer he stayed in the coma, the more concerned Dr. Fleming became.

Melanie was at his bedside, stroking his hand. The kids had gone to get something to eat and Claude was in a meeting. She talked to Alan about all the funny things she remembered during their childhood, the pranks he used to pull on his teachers and the time he taught her to swim. She told him how much she loved and needed him and she told him about her and Claude from the very beginning.

She slipped her hand into his cool one. "So you have to wake up, Al. I can't think about my own life while yours is connected to tubes and machines. I want you to see that I can be happy again, really happy, just the way you wanted me to be. And I want your blessing." She sniffed back her tears. She leaned over the rail and kissed his cheek. His long, strong fingers gently moved and squeezed hers.

For an instant she froze. She looked down at their joined hands. His fingers moved again.

"Al, Al, sweetie can you hear me? It's Mel." She tightened her grasp. "Al."

His eyelids fluttered. A soft groan passed across his lips.

Melanie reached for the buzzer and frantically pressed it to call for the nurse. Seconds later, the nurse was at the bedside.

"He's waking up. He grabbed my hand. He's waking up."

"Let me check him." She listened to his heart and shone a light in his eyes. She looked across at Melanie and smiled. "He's coming around."

Alan groaned again. His eyes opened then closed. He tried to move but the exertion seemed too much.

"Just relax, Mr. Harte," the nurse said, placing a gentle hand on his chest. She pressed the intercom above his bed. "Paging Dr. Fleming. Paging Dr. Fleming. Room 817."

Shortly, Dr. Fleming rushed into the room. He did an overall assessment, checked the monitors and IV lines. He gave the nurse some instructions on the change in medication and noted it in the chart. Then he focused on Melanie, who was trapped between elation and fear. Joy that her brother was coming around and dread about what that would mean for him when he did.

He walked Melanie away from the bed. "It looks like he's waking. It may take a little while longer. It really doesn't happen the way it does on television." He smiled benignly. "It could be any minute, a few hours or another day. He's trying to wake from a very, very deep sleep and that process happens in degrees. What you saw are the first signs. His pupils respond to light, which is a good indicator. In the meantime we will have to wait and see."

"Thank you, doctor," she managed to say.

"I know this is difficult, but try to be patient. Keep talking to him."

Melanie nodded and the doctor walked out. She turned back toward her brother.

"I'm going to bathe him now. If you could step out for a few minutes."

"Sure."

The nurse drew the curtain around the bed as Melanie walked out into the hall. She continued down the corridor to the vending machine. The elevator doors opened and out stepped Rafe Lawson.

He looked toward his left, trying to match the room numbers to the paper in his hand.

"Rafe?"

He turned in her direction and walked toward her. "How is he?"

"He's hanging in there. It looks like he's waking up."

Rafe nodded as she spoke, bringing him up to date on what had transpired.

"And how are you?" he asked, zeroing in on her taut expression.

"As well as can be expected. What are you doing here? How did you know where to find us?"

"You forget who my father is." He smiled. "I would have come sooner but I couldn't get away." He paused. "Alan is a good guy. I've been in his company on many occasions. He'll come through this."

She got a cup of coffee from the vending machine and they walked together to the lounge.

"I really appreciate you coming here, Rafe. That was truly nice of you."

"Quiet as it's kept, I really am a nice guy. I just have a lot of fun playing the rogue."

"That you do." She laughed lightly.

"Listen, I know this may not be the right time, but—"

She held up her hand, cutting him off. "Rafe, there can't be anything between us. There just can't for a lot of reasons, which have nothing to do with your incredible charm," she said to soften the blow. "It won't work. I'm sorry."

He smiled as if he'd just won a lotto. "I'm mighty glad you feel that way, cher. All that coming on to you was my game playing. I wanted to prove my father wrong and push your buttons in the process. Although," he lowered his voice and his eyes sparkled, "you are kinda sexy." He winked. "But for now, I like my life just the way that it is. I'm sure one of these days some wonderful woman is going to come along and slip a ring on my finger. But until then I'm going to enjoy myself. I love women. I think they are the most beautiful, extraordinary creatures that God created. And I want to meet as many of them as I can."

She shook her hand and laughed. "So all this time you were simply putting us all through our paces."

"Guilty as charged."

"What is your father going to say?"

"Same thing he always says, 'Son when are you ever gonna settle down with a good woman like your mama—God rest her soul?'" he mimicked in the pitch-perfect cadence of his powerful father.

Melanie couldn't help but laugh, the first time she'd laughed in days, and she fully understood the magnetic charm of Raford Lawson.

He took her hand. "Is there anything that I can do for you and your family?"

"No. I appreciate the offer, but we're doing okay."

He nodded then frowned. "Where are you staying?"

Her heart thumped. She shifted a bit in her seat.

"Claude Montgomery opened his house to us. We've been staying there. He was the one that called, arranged for us to get down here in record time," she rambled on.

He patted her hand. "It's okay. You don't have to explain."

She glanced down at the floor.

"Claude is a good man,"

She looked across at him. He was smiling.

"And if I didn't know better, I'd think he had a thing for you."

She swallowed. "Why would you think that?"

"I saw the way he looked at you on the dance floor that night at the embassy. A man knows when another man wants a woman."

Her face heated to near explosion.

He slowly stood. "Don't make him wait too long. D.C. is a tough town. The ratio of women to men is like ten to one." He winked. "I love those odds." He leaned down and kissed the top of her head. "You take care of yourself and you call if you need anything. Ever. Promise?"

"I promise."

He moved to go and she reached out and grabbed his hand. He turned halfway.

"Thank you."

"Always want to make the ladies happy." He walked to the door and met up with Vincent, Veronica and Jessica on the other side of the glass window. They talked for a few minutes. Rafe looked back at her and waved, then walked off.

The trio joined their aunt, who quickly brought them up to date on what had happened in their absence. They were so excited that everyone was talking at once. But it was Jessica's comment posed as a question that filtered above the others.

"Aunt Mel, you have two of the most gorgeous men hovering around you like bees to honey."

All eyes turned to their aunt.

"What? People care. Is something wrong with that?"

"I've seen the way Mr. Montgomery looks at you when you aren't looking," Jessica said.

"Me too," Veronica chirped.

"It's okay for you to have a life, Aunt Mel," Vincent added.

"You've made the business your life ever since Uncle Steven died," Jessica said. "On the surface you have this fantastic life and you take care of everyone and everything. You should have someone in your life to take care of you for a change."

"So when are you going to tell him?" Veronica asked.

"Tell who what?"

"Mr. Montgomery," Jessica filled in.

"Yeah, when are you going to tell him how you feel?" Vincent asked.

Melanie was totally flabbergasted. What did they actually know and when? She fumbled around for the words that couldn't find their way to her lips.

"We know," Veronica said.

"For quite some time," Jessica added. "Only a woman who cares about a man acts all weird like you do when they are around."

Melanie lowered her head and smiled. They weren't a team of matchmakers for no reason.

"And Mr. Lawson acting all hot and bothered around you just made it more interesting to watch," Vincent said.

Melanie opened her mouth to offer a weak protest just as the nurse stuck her head in the door. "He's awake."

His voice was raspy and his words halted, but his smile was unmistakable. The doctors wanted to run a few tests to see if there was any residual damage done to the brain because of the temporary loss of oxygen.

"All the signs are good," Dr. Fleming said, taking Melanie to the side. "He has a bit of a road ahead of him for a month or two, but he should recover well. He's going to need some help for the next few weeks. I know that he travels a great deal and lives alone."

"He's going to stay with me. I'll make sure that he gets whatever he needs."

"Good. If all of the tests come back satisfactory, I think he can go home in a few days."

"Thank you, doctor," she squeezed his arm. "Thank you for everything."

He offered a tight smile and walked off down the hall. Melanie drew in a long breath of relief. Her brother was stubbornly independent and she knew he would try to convince her that he could manage. But before she could even contemplate taking her nieces and nephew up on what they'd said about her having her own life and not taking care of others, she was going to see to the full recovery of her brother. It couldn't be any other way.

As soon as they were finished with their visit, Melanie sent Claude a text to inform him of the good news. He promised to get home as soon as he could so they all could celebrate. Her heart filled and she couldn't wait.

Chapter 16

The family stayed at the hospital, taking turns sitting with Alan until the nurse kicked them out, telling them that her patient needed his rest if he was planning on going home in a few days. They didn't need any more pushing.

When they arrived back at Claude's home he was already there and had sent out for Thai food for dinner. The air itself smelled edible.

"Oh my goodness, I'm starved," Jessica moaned, peeking into the containers.

"There's plenty. I guess I should have checked to see if you guys liked Thai."

"Right about now, I would eat a shoebox," Vincent joked.

They filed out to put away their things, leaving Melanie and Claude in the kitchen.

"You've got to be thrilled," he said.

"Oh you have no idea." She lowered herself into a chair. "I feel as if a boulder has been lifted." She slowly shook her head. I don't know what I would have done…"

"Thankfully, it's not an issue. In a few days Alan will be out of the hospital."

"I can't thank you enough for all that you've done. For being there."

"You don't have to thank me. I wanted to. Alan is my dear friend. And you…" his gaze danced over her face. "I would do anything that you needed."

His eyes drew her to him and she slowly stood. They were inches apart, close enough to hear the pound of each other's hearts.

"Mel…"

They jumped apart at the sound of voices and approaching footsteps but not before Jessica—the first one through the door—captured the deer in the headlights look on their faces.

Melanie moved away and tried to find someplace for her gaze to land. "I'm going to go and get cleaned up," she announced. "Just be sure to save some for me." She made a beeline for her room.

Jessica looked from one to the other with a knowing smirk.

* * *

Melanie got out of the clothes she'd been in all day, took a hot, refreshing shower, and changed into a T-shirt and jeans, scrubbed her face clean and ran a brush through her hair. She didn't know why she felt so awkward around her family in front of Claude, she mused, looking at her reflection in the mirror. She was a grown woman and they were adults. They were all in the business of love and romance. But this was different, it was private and personal and scary and she wasn't quite ready to share that with the world until she had it all figured out in her head.

She had strong feelings for Claude. Feelings that came out of nowhere with an intensity that shook her. For so long she'd kept up this wall between her and the world, blocking her ability to connect with anyone on a truly intimate level. But with Claude it was different. Different from the moment she saw him, and she couldn't help but laugh at how their first meeting was like a page from a romance novel that she'd read voraciously as a teen. That kind of instant attraction didn't happen in real life, she'd always said. But it did and it had happened to her, short circuiting all of her preconceived notions.

And of course she'd had sexual encounters before, been made love to before, been in love and married. But again, with Claude it was new, vibrant and different. She didn't want to be one of those women who fell in love with the sex because it was so earthshakingly good. But it was good. It was mind-blowing and life-altering. Most of all it was sincere. She'd not just given Claude her body, she'd opened a part of her soul. And that was something she had not ever done, not even with Steven, who she'd loved dearly.

She was older now and hopefully wiser. She knew what she needed, had imagined what she'd wanted, but for a long time she thought it was all wishful thinking. And then all of her needs and imaginings appeared across the dance floor embodied in Claude Montgomery and she hadn't been the same person since.

She placed the brush on the dresser and walked back out to the kitchen.

Everyone was seated around the table finishing up their meal.

"I've decided to take my sister and cousin out for the evening," Vincent announced. "Do a little celebrating."

"Oh," she managed to be a bit surprised at the sudden decision.

"Claude said we could use his Suburban. So we're going to drive into Georgetown to see if we can catch a late jazz show."

"And, uh, if it gets too late…we might just find a hotel or something and crash," Veronica added.

"Yeah, the hotels should be opening up now. The conventions are over," Jessica said. "I checked."

Melanie folded her arms. Her lips were pinched together. She had the distinct feeling that there was a conspiracy against her by the innocent-looking trio who stared back at her wide-eyed and unassuming.

"Seems as if you all have it figured out."

"Yep," they chorused and started clearing the table just as Claude walked back into the room.

"We may or may not be back tonight, Claude," Vincent said. "Will it be a problem if I don't get your ride back to you until morning?"

"No, not at all," he said haltingly, not sure what had transpired. "I don't have any plans for the morning and I have the other car if need be."

"Great. Well, you two enjoy yourselves," Victoria said, her mischievous smile giving away more than her words.

"Yeah, don't wait up." Jessica kissed her aunt's cheek and whispered, "It's about you now, Aunt Mel. Don't blow it."

Shortly after, with keys jingling, shouts of laughter and cries of "hurry up" and doors opening and closing, Claude and Melanie found themselves alone in the big rambling house.

"That was like being swept up in a whirlwind," Claude said over his rumbling laughter.

"Yes, they can be a force to be reckoned with,

especially when they band together, which they decided to do tonight."

"So I gather."

The table separated them. Melanie ran her tongue across her lips. "So," she said on a breath, "have you eaten yet?"

"No. But I just had my own burst of inspiration."

Her eyes widened. "And what might that be?"

"You deserve to celebrate, too."

She held up her hand. "I'm really not up to going out, if that's what you had in mind."

"Nope. Something better, I'm going to bring the celebration to you, right here. Food, wine, entertainment, good conversation…what do you say?" He spread his arms.

She giggled. "I'm really interested in the entertainment part."

He came around the table and put his arms around her waist. "Let the show begin. And since I'm no longer a client of The Society…" He leaned down and kissed her long and slow, savoring the sweetness of her mouth, the feel of her full lips against his. He pulled her body flush against his and the electric sensation charged through his veins, filling his erection that was so hard and throbbing that it was almost painful.

Her arms wrapped around his broad back, her fingers gliding up and down his spine. She felt his need that matched hers in intensity until her head spun and her knees grew weak.

"I want you. I want to make love to you. Now," he whispered urgently against her mouth. "But I want to savor every moment." His strong fingers coursed along her sides, his thumbs brushing across the undersides of her breasts. With great reluctance he let her go, kissing her lightly one last time. "Come on, let's eat. I have a feeling we are going to need all of our strength."

Melanie couldn't remember the last time she was fully aware of actually being seduced. She knew that when she dealt with clients, especially those whose skills in the art of love and romance were suspect, she always insisted that they take their time, pay attention to the needs, wants and responses of the woman before they moved from one step to the next.

Where men's stimulation was much more visual and physical, women's arousal began in their minds. Play with their minds, talk to their minds, stir their imagination, was what she always advised. And if she didn't know better, she'd swear that Claude was her prize pupil. But his attention to her wasn't trained or coaxed—it was as natural as his smile or the spark in his eyes. When he touched her hand or her cheek, it wasn't choreographed.

As they worked side by side at the counter in the kitchen spooning their food onto plates and popping them in the microwave, it felt to Melanie as if this was what they'd always done together.

He talked to her about his day at the office as they sat next to each other on the couch, soft music from the high-tech stereo system filling out the background. He told her of some of the personnel issues he'd had to deal with and the education reform bill that kept getting torn apart.

"There are really good people in office who want to do the right thing by the people of this country, but they are outgunned and outnumbered," he said, taking a bite of his food. "More wine?" he asked, holding up the bottle.

"Sure, thanks." She held out her glass, then sipped her wine. "What got you into politics?"

"Good question. I suppose it all began when I was a kid. I grew up in Algiers in Louisiana. We had it tough as a family and a community. A family down the road from us lost everything in a fire. The community came together to raise money for food, clothes and getting them a place to live. When I saw how genuinely happy they were for all the help, I guess I got the bug.

"I joined organizations in school, helped out in food banks and when I got to college I majored in political science. I met Senator Lawson about ten years ago at a fundraiser. When his chief of staff position opened up, he offered it to me."

"But you're not actually making policy."

"No, but I have the ear of all those who do. That's where the real power is."

"Hmm. You're right." She looked at him, tipping her head to the side. "I suppose I never looked at it quite that way."

"I have the ear of the folks on the ground and I pass their message along to those who matter. I work really hard at getting people what they want." He waited a beat. "What do you want, Melanie Harte?"

She was thoughtful for a moment. "For a long while I thought that all I wanted was to make everyone else happy, follow in the footsteps of my grandmother and my mother. It filled my days, my thoughts, and… many of my nights." She took a sip of wine, then placed the glass on the coffee table. She curled her feet beneath her. "I've watched so many relationships bloom and grow into something beautiful. I watched from the sidelines for years. And it made me happy. It really did. But recently I realized that although it made me happy, it didn't fulfill me. It was as if I was on this never-ending beautiful rainbow, but there was no pot of gold at the end for me." She turned her head and looked into his searching gaze. "And then there you were." She smiled shyly. "I have a confession to make."

"Do I want to hear it?"

"Just listen." She scooted closer. "When you were being set up for your dates, even though I knew the women were perfect for you, I secretly hoped that they wouldn't work out because if they didn't, even if I couldn't be with you I still could be in a way because you would keep coming back to try again."

"We wasted a lot of time avoiding what was on our minds. But I totally understand the dilemma you were faced with. To you, you'd violated your ethics. And I know how important your business and your reputation are to you. I admire that, even though it did get me kicked to the curb."

They both laughed.

"I'm sorry about that."

"I'm sorry about a lot of things, too. Like jumping to conclusions about you and Rafe Lawson."

"You're kidding!"

He shook his head and told her about the day he'd driven into town and saw them together. "My very vivid imagination took over from there."

She laughed softly. "Rafe did have his own agenda, but it wasn't about me."

"*My* agenda is about you," he said, his tone so low it was barely above a whisper. "All of it."

"Is it?"

He cupped her chin in his palm and drew her close. "Every inch of it." He took her hands. "Tonight is going to be about new beginnings." She tried to see beyond the depths of his eyes to get a hint at his meaning. "Claude Montgomery. I work for Senator Lawson," he said with all due sincerity.

The corners of her mouth tugged upward. "Melanie Harte. It's nice to meet you. I've heard wonderful things about you from my brother."

"Would you like to dance?"

"I'd love to."

He brought her to her feet and guided her to the center of the living room. She moved into his arms as if it was the most natural place in the world to be and rested her head against his chest. He held her close as they swayed to Leela James' sultry rendition of "A Change Is Gonna Come."

> …it's been a loooong, a long time coming but I know a change is gonna come. Oh yes it will.

They held each other, moving together in perfect harmony as the music switched from Leela to Luther to Kem to the Whispers.

Melanie felt as if she'd been transported. It had been so long since she felt this kind of peace. Claude had the power to soothe her in a way that she couldn't explain. It was his own sense of assuredness that radiated around him.

"This is what I've been searching for," he said softly against her hair. "This sense of calm."

She looked up at him. "It's like you're reading my mind. I was thinking the same thing."

"Were you thinking about this too?" He lowered his head and tenderly brushed his lips against hers, and the contact, as always, was a shock to his system, an awakening as if he'd been jerked from sleep.

Melanie linked her fingers around his neck and savored the pleasure of his mouth against hers. Lightly she brushed her tongue across his lips, tapping the doorway for entrance. He opened for her in a way that she longed to open for him—hot, wet and inviting.

The music swirled around them and even though the air was on full blast it could not compete with the heat that they stirred in each other.

Claude tightened his hold on her, sealing her body to his, the hard throbbing between his legs seeking a home between hers.

Melanie shuddered with pleasure as his tongue dipped and cut a hot trail along the cord of her neck, sending shimmers of delight racing through her body. She clung to him, pressing her want against his need.

"If I were ten years younger, I'd say here's the floor, let's go for it," he whispered roughly in her ear.

"Hmm, you and me both." She tore herself away

and grabbed his hand. "Can I interest you in my boudoir?"

He grinned wickedly. "You can interest me in anything."

She pulled him toward her room down the hall, as they laughed, kissed and hugged like teenagers along the way. Claude pushed the door open and they tumbled inside, finding their way to the queen-sized bed.

Melanie tugged at the bottom of his T-shirt and pulled it up and over his head. Her lips circled his nipples, then trailed a path down his chest to his belly, where she loosened the knot on his sweat pants and pushed them down over his thighs. He kicked them aside and focused all of his attention on her.

To Melanie everything seemed to be in slow motion, and she captured every sensation, every image. His hands and mouth were like hot coals everywhere that they landed, searing her skin. When he slipped her bra off her shoulders and suckled her hardened nipples, she cried out with pleasure. His touch was feather light as it grazed across her exposed flesh, the sensations were so intense that it clouded her thinking.

Claude eased her back against the thick pillows and began a slow and steady exploration of every inch of her. When he reached her navel, her stomach quivered. He went further, running his tongue along the band of her panties. For a moment she stiffened, but he soothed her thighs with long-loving strokes until she was pliant once again.

He inched her panties down over her hips, along her thighs and her legs then tossed them to the floor. He began at her ankles, kissing and nibbling, working his way up to her inner thighs. Ever so gently he pushed her thighs apart and pressed his face longingly at her center. He inhaled the sweet scent of her that had his erection jumping at the new assault on his senses.

He ran his wet tongue across the hard knot of her clit and felt it twitch and jerk in response.

Melanie gripped handfuls of the sheet while he delved deeper, licking and teasing, driving her wild as her hips moved of their own accord, seeking out all that he had to offer.

Her moans filled the air as he cupped her hips to pull her closer so that he could go deeper, gathering her essence. Her stomach muscles fluttered and jumped. Her inner thighs trembled. A blinding heat infused her as the pleasure built to a crescendo. Her hips lifted off the bed. Her head thrashed back and forth against the pillows. She tried to cry out but the feeling was so powerful and intense that it stole the sounds from her throat. Stars burst from behind her lids as the lava-like explosion began at her curled toes, jettisoned up her legs and erupted with such force that she felt her body soar to the heavens, among the moon and stars then slowly, exquisitely return to earth.

Low moans slipped from her lips as Claude tenderly worked his way up her body, resting his weight between her parted thighs.

He brushed damp strands of hair away from her face and ran his finger across her sleek brows. "Look at me."

Her eyes fluttered open and she floated into the depths of his dark eyes. He took her hand and stretched it down between them, wrapping her fingers around him. His eyes squeezed shut for an instant as the thrill of her touch shot through him.

He focused on her again. "Put me inside of you. As much or as little as you want."

"All of you," she managed to say.

"Then show me what you want."

She spread her thighs and bent her knees, keeping her fingers wrapped around him as she stroked him up and down. She brought the thick tip of him to her wet opening and they both moaned in anticipation. She bumped her hips against him, letting just the tip of him get beyond her doorway and then pulled away. She did it again and again, and each time she let him in a little bit further, letting him stay a little bit longer until she'd captured the length of him and she held him in place with the grip of her womanly muscle until he couldn't take the sublime torture a moment longer.

He slid his arms under her thighs and pushed them open and up around his neck, compelling her to now succumb to his will. She was totally helpless. Completely open. Absolutely ready.

He wanted to rush. He wanted to plunge. He wanted to drive home his raging need. But he wanted it to last. This unspeakable ecstasy. So he took her slow and deep and steady, moving within her like the waves of the ocean, rising and falling and rushing to shore, then surging back.

His groans of pleasure, his need for fulfillment was so powerful that they set off another series of explosions within Melanie.

She whimpered and trembled as her climax overtook her. She felt a sensation, from the soles of her feet to the top of her head. She was on fire. Tears slid from her eyes and Claude kissed them away and then her lips, his tongue doing to her mouth what his body was doing to hers. In and out. In and out.

She offered up her aching breasts that she cupped in her hand and let him feast on their sweetness. And that was his undoing. He knew he was incapable of holding back a moment longer as the hot, slick fire inside her ignited the powder keg that stiffened and lengthened, shooting off a mind-blowing stream that rocked them both, dousing the firestorm until it smoldered into tiny embers waiting to be stoked once again.

Claude lowered her legs as his weight eased down on her. He buried his face in her neck, too weak to move.

Melanie tenderly caressed his back. She had no words to describe what had happened to her, to them. It was surreal. She didn't know that the body could endure that kind of intense pleasure without breaking into a million tiny pieces. It was frightening in its power. And she relished every exhilarating moment.

She pressed her lips to his neck and kissed him softly before drifting off to sleep with the fullness of Claude still resting inside of her.

She wasn't sure how long she'd slept, only that her dreams had been sweet and filled with visions of her and Claude. But something had awakened her, stirred her, incited her. Her eyes fluttered open and her body came alive. Claude was tenderly suckling her breasts, his fingers exploring her depths. Her breath caught when his finger found and pressed against the epicenter of her being. Her hips arched. The cords of her neck tightened. He pressed again, teased it, until she was one live wire and then he entered her over and again until they were spent and weak.

They slept entwined until the sun rose on another day.

Chapter 17

The sounds of clanging pots and laughter stirred them from their satiated slumber. Claude groaned and covered his eyes against the sun, draping his other arm around Melanie.

"Is that the kids?" she whispered.

"Unless we have laughing burglars who like to cook," he said, his voice still thick with sleep.

"Oh God, how long have they been home? Do you think they heard me last night?"

"Don't worry about it," he said, as he kissed the back of her neck. "The whole neighborhood heard you."

She gasped and swatted him on the hip. "Not funny. You could have been a one-man choir yourself."

He chuckled and nuzzled closer. "I'll sing a tune for you any day, baby."

She couldn't help laughing. Over her giggles she asked him how he planned to get out of there without anyone seeing him.

"Now that's a tough one. But since it's my house, I can pretty much go and come as I please."

"Claude," she said, dragging out his name into two syllables. "I'm serious. What will they think?"

He pushed up to a halfway-sitting position and rested his head on his hand. "It'll confirm what they already know…that I'm crazy about their aunt and I spent the night in her bed to prove it to her."

She huffed.

"Want me to prove it again?" He slid his hand down between her thighs.

"Stop it," she said without much sincerity.

"If you promise to be quiet…" he nibbled at her neck "…I'll do it nice and slow." He moved on top of her, spreading her thighs with a sweep of his knee.

"You drive a really hard bargain," she moaned.

"But I thought you liked hard bargains…" He pushed deep inside of her, stealing the air from her lungs.

* * *

When they emerged more than an hour later, Veronica was at the kitchen table finishing off a glass of orange juice and reading the morning paper.

"Well, good morning, you two." She beamed at them. "And how was your evening?"

"Mine was incredible," Claude said, before linking his arm around Melanie's waist. He looked down at her and in his eyes he wanted her to see that it was okay.

A slow, sweet smile moved across her mouth. "Yes, it was," she said softly.

"Well, amen," Veronica answered enthusiastically. "You guys hungry? There's food in the oven. We were going to head over to the hospital in about an hour."

"Good. You three can take the Suburban. I'll bring your aunt in my car."

"Thanks." She rose from the table and took her cup to the sink.

Melanie came beside her to pour a cup of coffee.

"You look radiant, Aunt Mel," she said quietly.

Melanie turned to her niece. "I feel radiant," she admitted.

Veronica kissed her on the cheek. "He's a lucky man," she whispered in her ear before walking out.

Melanie leaned against the counter and Claude came to stand beside her.

"See that wasn't so bad." He smiled down at her.

She glanced up at him and felt all girly inside. "No it wasn't." She drew in a breath. "How soon will you be ready to head over to the hospital?"

"Give me about a half hour. I want to make some phone calls."

"Sure, hopefully there's more good news today."

"There will be. Can't you tell that the stars have finally aligned?" He kissed the tip of her nose and walked out.

They certainly have, she thought, grinning inside as she watched him from the back. They certainly have.

When they arrived at the hospital, Dr. Fleming was just coming out of Alan's room.

"Good morning, doctor," Melanie greeted. "How is he today?"

"He rested very well last night. We're going to run some tests this morning and start him on soft foods. If he has a good day and night and the results come back the way I hope, I think we can discharge him tomorrow."

Melanie pressed her hands to her face to keep from screaming with joy. "Thank you, thank you."

The doctor genuinely smiled for the first time

since they'd met. "You are quite welcome. He's still in a weak state, so not too much excitement."

"Of course. Whatever he needs, whatever it takes."

The doctor nodded and walked off.

The entire family melded together in a family hug, a hug that included Claude, each saying their own little prayer of thanks. Finally they separated, sniffing back tears of relief.

"You all go on in. I'll wait," Melanie offered.

The trio filed inside and Melanie and Claude walked over to the visitors' lounge.

"I guess you're going to talk to Alan today about his new living arrangements." Claude took a seat next to her.

"Not looking forward to that. He's going to want to be in his own house with his own things."

"I'm sure that if he puts up too much of a fight, the State Department can arrange for whatever he needs if he goes home."

"Where is home for my brother?" she asked. "He lives out of a suitcase and never stays anywhere long enough to call anyplace home. Not really."

"He seems to like it that way. No roots, nothing to hold him down."

"Hmm. That's going to have to change. At least for a while."

"I get the distinct feeling that you have no intention of taking no for an answer."

She crossed her legs. "You're absolutely right. On this I'm not going to budge. Whatever he needs I'll make sure he gets it…at home, with his family, where he belongs."

"The two of you are very much alike. Both of you have been consumed by your jobs."

She raised a brow. "I'd say that makes three of us." She pointed a finger at him.

He chuckled. "You're right. And it took something major for each of us to see what's really important. Living. Loving. Family."

The glow of a smile softened her mouth as she leaned toward him for a kiss.

The intrusive sound of someone clearing their throat pulled them apart. They turned in the direction of the door. Vincent, Veronica and Jessica were grinning like Cheshire cats.

Melanie slowly stood. "How is he?"

"Asking for you," Jessica offered.

Melanie turned to Claude. "You want to come in with me?"

"No you go. I can wait."

She walked toward the wall of grins and she would have sworn she heard her nephew ask what Claude's intentions were toward his aunt. She shuddered with laughter.

When she entered Alan's room, he was sitting up eating a cup of Jell-O. He saw her and his eyes lit up. In only a matter of days he'd gone from wan and weak-looking to almost his old self. Although he still looked a bit drawn, he didn't have that frightening sunken appearance like when she'd first arrived.

Melanie hurried over to his bed, dropping her purse in the chair. She leaned over the rails and pressed her face against his, rejoicing in his warmth.

She stepped back and really looked at him. "You scared me good this time, big bro."

"You know I'll do anything for attention. I needed a rest anyway," he said, trying to make light of what had almost taken him away from the people that he loved.

She dragged the chair closer to the bed, picked up her purse and sat down. "How are you feeling?"

"Like a pin cushion. And I'm starving. How do they expect a grown man to get his strength back on this?" He held up the wobbly red concoction.

Melanie giggled. "They want you to take it slow. One hurdle at a time. I'm sure they intend to feed you."

"Hmm," he grumbled.

"Yep, you're getting better."

He winked at her. "The doctor said I should be getting out of here by tomorrow."

"Yes, and I wanted to talk to you about that. You're

going to stay at my house until you're strong enough and the doctor gives his okay. I won't take no for an answer. So don't think about giving me a hard time. I'll arrange whatever you need," she rambled on, intent on beating him into submission with a barrage of words.

"Okay, okay, I give up."

Melanie stopped in mid sentence. She craned her neck and peered at him. "What?"

"I said, okay. I think it's a great idea."

She blinked several times to make sure she was looking at her brother and not some Stepford replacement. "I…well…that's great. You mean I don't have to spend the rest of the afternoon trying to convince you?"

"Nope. I turn myself over to your very capable hands."

She leaned back and tried to figure out what was really going on. "Why is this so easy? I was sure that you would put up a fight."

He drew in a long breath and pushed the tray aside. "These past couple of days, being here, being this close to dying, it made me think about things. The things that are important. Sure I love my freedom, the travel, the excitement and the challenge. But at the end of the day there's no one to share that with. I see my kids a couple of times a year, mostly just passing through. And I don't want that anymore.

"If it's never been clear to me before, it's clear to me now. Tomorrow is not promised. And you need to make each day count with the ones you love." He reached out and touched her cheek. "I've been thinking about putting in for a permanent station in New York, so that I can be closer to you all..."

As she listened to her brother remap his life, she was totally convinced in miracles.

Curled in Claude's strong arms that night, Melanie told him of her conversation with Alan.

"It was amazing," she said, caressing the smooth skin of his bare chest. "It's as if he is a totally different person."

"I'm sure he is, Mel. Coming that close to death is a revelation for anyone."

"You're right." She sighed. "So much has changed so quickly that it's hard to keep up. You and me, my brother."

"All good things," he said turning on his side to face her. "I wanted to talk to you about something."

Her pulse quickened. "Sure."

"I'm going to have to stay in D.C. for a while. There's a lot going on right now, especially with this being an election year for many of the senators."

Her spirits sunk. "Oh. Of course you have your job here."

"I'll call you every day. I promise. And the next

few weeks will fly by." He brushed his thumb across her lips.

"I know. And I'll have plenty to keep me busy." She tried to sound upbeat, but inside she felt like she was sinking. She'd just found her piece of happiness and she wasn't ready to let it go so soon, even for a little while. She knew it was selfish. She had her work and Claude had his. But for the first time in her life she wanted something *just* for Melanie and she didn't want to share it or part with it. She buried her face against his chest, seeking comfort from the steady beat of his heart.

The following morning, the family spent an hour with the doctor, who explained the medication, diet and exercise program that Alan had to strictly follow. He put them in touch with the visiting nurse service and said that he planned to contact Alan's private physician, as well.

With all of the technicalities out of the way they wheeled Alan out of the hospital and into a waiting government vehicle that would take them to the airport.

Claude had arranged for a nurse to fly with them, "just as a precaution," he'd said. He rode with them to the private landing strip.

"I'll call you tonight," he said, holding her close while the others boarded the plane. A light rain had begun to fall.

She nodded against his chest. He tilted her chin upward. "You make sure you take it easy. Don't let Alan run you ragged," he said with a grin.

"I won't. Are you sure you'll be down for the celebration?"

"Without a doubt. Don't worry about that. Don't worry about us."

She pressed her lips together, then forced a smile. "I'll try."

"They're waiting for you." He looked heavenward. "The weather is going to get worse before it gets better. You need to get going."

"I can't thank you enough for everything."

"I'm sure you'll figure out something." He kissed her lightly, then physically turned her in the direction of the plane. "Go. Go. I'll talk to you tonight."

"Okay," she shouted above a sudden gust of wind. She ran across the tarmac and up the steps. She turned one final time and waved goodbye before stepping on board.

Claude waited and watched until the plane disappeared among the clouds. He turned up his coat collar and strode toward the waiting vehicle.

The flight was bumpy all the way as they flew into a thunderstorm that had already hit New York and was working its way south. The roller coaster effect was taking its toll on all of them as the hour and a half flight turned into three while they were continually detoured as the storm worsened.

"We're going to have to land in Philadelphia," the pilot said over the intercom. "The storm is getting worse and we're running low on fuel. I got the okay to land and I'm heading in. We should be on the ground in twenty minutes."

A collective groan echoed through the plane.

"Are we going to have to stay overnight in Philly?" Jessica asked.

"I hope not. I'll ask the pilot." Vincent got up from his seat and inched toward the cockpit as the plane swayed back and forth. Vincent returned shortly with a bit of good news.

"The pilot says that the storm has passed through New York and should go by Philadelphia in an hour or two. So hopefully after refueling and a short layover we can be on our way."

"Thank goodness," Veronica said.

Vincent returned to his seat and leaned toward Melanie. "Are you okay? You don't look too good."

Her stomach seesawed. "Don't feel all that great. The turbulence must have gotten to me." She willed her stomach to be calm as the plane rose and fell. She shut her eyes and breathed deeply through her mouth.

"Try to rest. We should be landing soon." He glanced over at his father, who had been sound asleep for most of the flight. "We'll have to tell Dad all about it."

By the time they landed, Melanie's head was pounding and her stomach was swirling. The captain walked into the passenger compartment.

"We should be on the ground for about an hour. If you want to get off and hang out inside the terminal you can. But I need everyone back here in forty-five minutes. Once they give us the go-ahead we have a short window to take off. If we miss it, we may be stuck here overnight. They predict another front is coming this way."

"I'm going to get out," Vincent announced. His sister and cousin joined him.

Melanie rested her head back against the seat, thankful that they were on solid ground even if her stomach told her otherwise.

"Are you all right, Ms. Harte? You don't look well," the nurse said, taking Vincent's seat opposite her.

"Just the bumpy ride," she said from between clenched teeth.

The nurse reached over and touched her damp forehead. "No fever. Do you have chills or aches?"

She shook her head.

"Do you normally get air sick?"

"No. I've been on planes all my life."

"Hmm."

Melanie opened her eyes to see the nurse staring at her. "What do you think it is?"

"If you're not coming down with something and you're accustomed to flying...maybe you should visit your doctor when you get home." She gave her a knowing smile, patted her hand then returned to check on her dozing patient.

Melanie frowned. Then her thoughts began to scramble as the nurse's words replayed in her head and the look she had on her face when she suggested that she see her doctor. She tried to think, but the unthinkable began to dominate her thoughts. No.

Her heart started to race and a line of perspiration ran around her forehead. No.

She thought about that first night. That night with Claude. They hadn't used protection. The thought had unnerved her afterward, but then she'd tossed it out of her head with so many other things crowding into her life. No. She tried to count but the numbers got all screwed up. She pulled her cell phone out of her purse and fumbled for the calendar application. Last Friday's date was highlighted. That was a week ago. That's when she should have gotten her period. But she didn't.

Her heart was thumping so loud she couldn't hear herself think. Her fingers began to shake. It was probably all of the anxiety, the party, then Alan... That's all that it was and as soon as she calmed down and got her life back on track everything would be fine.

She drew in a long deep breath and put her phone back in her purse. She turned to stare out of the window. Everything was going to be fine. It had to be.

the plane and left the strap around everything
would be okay.

Before he left, Vincent handed out her room
key at the desk. She turned to stare at the eleva-
tors. Everything was going to be fine. It was...

Chapter 18

Melanie was subdued for the rest of the flight to
New York. In the car she barely uttered a word.

Veronica tapped on Melanie's bedroom door.
"Come in."

"I was getting ready to head home. Vincent's gone
home. Dad's asleep. His nurse is settled in the room
across from him. I'm going to drop Jess off on my
way, but I wanted to check on you first. Are you sure
you're feeling okay?"

"Yeah, sweetie, I'm fine. I think everything is
finally catching up with me, that's all. Nothing for
you to worry about." She forced a reassuring smile
across her face.

"If you're sure."

"Yes, I'm perfectly fine. Go home and get some sleep in your own bed."

"I like the sound of that. See you in the morning. You get some rest."

"I will, sweetheart. Good night. Set the alarm on your way out."

Melanie took a long shower then went to check on her brother, who was resting comfortably. Crawling under the covers she closed her eyes against the impossible. But of course it was possible, silly. You didn't use protection. She groaned in concert with the ringing phone. It was Claude and as much as she wanted to hear his voice she didn't want to talk to him now.

"Hey, baby, you all get settled?"

"Yes." She told him about the delays they encountered and that she was really tired.

"Sure. You get some rest. I'll call you tomorrow."

"Great. Good night."

She hung up the phone. Her heart was suddenly so heavy it felt as if it weighed a ton. She slid down under the covers and tried to sleep. First thing in the morning she was taking a trip to the pharmacy.

Melanie was up before the sun. She'd barely slept through the night. As soon as she sat up, her stomach revolted and she darted to the bathroom. Trying to compose herself she splashed cold water on her face. Maybe it was a stomach virus, she told herself. Because thirty-six-year-old, successful, unmarried business women didn't just pop up pregnant. Taking a deep breath, she slowly stood. The stores wouldn't be open for a couple of hours. The waiting was agony.

As soon as it was reasonable, Melanie advised the nurse that she had to run out for a little while but would be back within the hour.

Driving into town seemed to take an eternity. A part of her wanted the road never to end and another part couldn't get there fast enough. She found a parking space across the street from the pharmacy and suddenly wished she'd put on something to hide her appearance. Suppose someone she knew saw her? What would they think? What would she say? For a moment she hesitated, doubting her actions. It would be much more discreet if she simply went to her doctor. But she didn't think she could endure the not knowing. This could all be a simple mistake. But her rolling stomach told her otherwise.

As nonchalantly as she could she browsed the feminine products aisle until she found what she was looking for. She read the information on the back. Sounded simple enough. She looked around to see if anyone was watching. Only she and a woman she didn't recognize were in the store. She hurried to the cashier, paid for her kit and rushed out.

By the time she got behind the wheel of her car her heart was racing out of control. She felt as if she had just succeeded on some covert mission. Willing herself to calm down, she put the car in gear and headed back home.

An hour later, her suspicions were confirmed. The little blue line was positive. What was she going to do now?

Claude couldn't seem to concentrate on the meeting he was sitting in on. The words blurred in his head, not making sense. All night he felt unsettled, as if something was wrong. He started feeling that way right after speaking with Melanie. She didn't sound right. She sounded distant and detached, not like the woman he'd spent the past week with, who opened her heart and soul to him and he in return.

He tried to pass it off that she was tired and that the strain of the past week had finally taken its toll. But his gut told him it was something else. What that something was he couldn't tell.

He checked his watch for the tenth time. The meeting was scheduled to wrap up in another twenty minutes. The time couldn't go by fast enough. He needed to talk to Melanie. He needed to hear her voice and be reassured that everything was all right with her and with them.

Was she having second thoughts about having plunged headfirst into a relationship with him? Did she think she did the right thing? He should have told her how he felt, what had been going through his head and his heart, but he didn't want to scare her off. He didn't want her to think that he was telling her that he was falling in love with her, simply because the sex was so incredible.

It was more than that. It was everything. His thoughts were consumed with her and how he could make her happy. He felt as if he'd fallen from the moment that they met. He plunged headfirst into the depths of her eyes and she took over his soul. Everything he did from the time they met was with her in mind. Even when he got crazy about Rafe.

He should have told her exactly how happy and complete she made him feel. Something he didn't think he would ever experience again.

"Your body is here but your head has been somewhere else all morning."

Claude looked up at Senator Lawson. He shook his head to clear it. "Sorry about that. Was it that obvious?" He closed his leather folder and stood, noticing that only he and the senator were in the room.

"Only to the people that really know you, like everyone in the room." He chuckled lightly and slapped him on the back. "Everything all right with you? You're not coming down with something?"

"No. I'm fine. Just a little tired."

"Well, you be sure to take care of yourself. We have a lot on our agenda and I'm going to need you to be in top form."

"Yes, sir."

Senator Lawson gave a short nod and strode out.

Once he spoke to Melanie he would be fine, he thought as he walked out. He just needed to hear that sparkle in her voice to know that everything was all right and then he could loosen the knot that gripped his insides.

By midday she was feeling like herself again. The nausea had passed and her head had cleared. Maybe the test was wrong, she tried to convince herself as she walked down the hall to her brother's room. She peeked her head in and he beckoned her inside.

"Hey, sweetie, how are you feeling today?" She crossed the room. He was sitting up in the chair by the window looking even better today than the day before.

"Slept like a baby." He grinned, and that old smile was back.

She sat down on the window ledge and looked out onto the moss-covered bluffs, then back at her brother.

"Seems like I should be asking you how you're doing. What's wrong?"

"Nothing." She forced a smile.

Alan made a face. "Don't lie to your big brother. What is it? Is it about Claude?"

Her eyes widened in surprise. She sputtered something incoherent.

"You think I didn't know?" He smiled wickedly. "We fellas have to stick together."

She folded her arms defiantly. "Stick together about what?"

"About women, of course." He chuckled. "Don't look so put out. The man is crazy about you."

Her heart pounded. "How do you know that?"

"Because he told me. Besides a blind man can see the vibe between the two of you."

"He told you?" She didn't know whether to be appalled or to laugh with relief.

"Every chance he got that's all he talked about. I had to kind of stop him before he got to the juicy parts," he teased. "After all, you are my baby sister."

She jumped down from her perch on the window ledge and began to pace. She turned to her brother, her expression as bright as a Fourth of July fireworks display. "What did he say about me?"

Alan tossed his head back and laughed. "Us men have to have some secrets," he taunted her.

"Grrrr. If you weren't an invalid I would jump all over you!"

Alan laughed some more. "Lucky me."

She stopped pacing and planted her hands on her hips. "Why won't you tell me what he said? Can't you at least give me a tiny hint?" she whined.

"Why don't you ask him?" His smile was soft and loving. "I have a strong feeling that he's ready to tell you what's been on his mind."

But would he still feel the same way when she told him her news?

She returned to her room and put in a call to her doctor, insisting that she squeeze her in. It was an emergency. The nurse said she could have the last appointment of the day at six. Melanie assured her that she would be there. With that task aside she called Cynthia. She needed some girl talk and the ear and support of her best friend.

Vincent had taken the day off and Jessica and Veronica were busy going over some new files. She told them she was going out to run an errand and meet with Cynthia and that she would be back later in the evening.

She drove into town, stopped at the local bakery and picked up some fresh bread and rolls. Then she stopped in the florist and placed an order for a flower delivery. With those tasks out of the way she walked down to Cynthia's gallery.

The gallery was relatively quiet with only a smattering of visitors. Cynthia was just finishing up on the phone and waved Melanie over. She leaned across the counter and kissed Melanie's cheek.

"I knew from your call that something was wrong. And now it's in your face." She reached for her purse from beneath the counter. "What is it? Come on in back and we'll talk."

Just hearing Cynthia's gentle words of concern eased the tension that had a stronghold on Melanie's insides. She followed Cynthia to her back office. She closed the door and sat down on the comfortable love seat.

"First, how is Alan?"

"He is doing so much better. He was sitting up today. His nurse said that she's going to let him do some walking."

"Oh, thank God. I was so worried." She breathed a sigh of relief, then focused all of her attention on Melanie. "Now, what's going on with you?"

Melanie folded her hands in her lap and in measured words took Cynthia on the journey of her and Claude's worldwind affair, right up to the results she'd gotten that morning and Alan's intimation.

For a moment, Cynthia was completely speechless as she tried to process it all. "Girl, you don't have a relationship for decades and then when you do it's an Oprah moment."

Melanie didn't want to laugh but she couldn't help it. "Ain't that the truth?"

"I know you're torn right down the middle about everything right now. But let me ask you this one question: How do you feel about Claude? I mean really feel deep down in your soul?"

Her lips quivered as the intensity of what she felt for Claude tried to form words. She looked straight at her friend. "I'm in love with him."

Cynthia flipped through the magazines on the table and watched the women in various stages of pregnancy come in and out of the office. Just thinking about her friend as one of them gave her pause. She knew that Melanie would make a great mother. She'd spent her entire adult life taking care of others. She only wanted her to be happy and for Claude to be happy when he got the news.

She checked her watch. Melanie had been in with the doctor for more than half an hour. Now she was getting nervous. Just when she didn't think she could take the suspense a moment longer, Melanie emerged. She couldn't read her expression. She tossed the magazine onto the table.

"Well?" she said the instant Melanie was close enough.

Melanie hooked her arm through Cynthia's and ushered her toward the door.

"I'm not pregnant," she said once they'd stepped outside.

"What? But I thought…"

"I know. It's the same thing I said to my doctor who, after a thorough exam, assured me that I'm not pregnant, just late. She said that every now and then those little tests are wrong."

They walked arm in arm toward Melanie's car. "She went on to give me a thorough lecture on safe sex." She snickered. "I felt like I was twelve. 'You should know better Melanie. There are a lot worse things you get besides becoming pregnant,'" she mimicked.

Cynthia laughed. "Ouch."

Melanie stopped and opened her purse for Cynthia to see. She looked inside. The entire bottom was filled with condoms in a rainbow of colors and flavors. They both cracked up laughing.

"So how do you feel about finding out that you're not pregnant?" Cynthia gently asked while Melanie drove her home.

Melanie took a deep breath. "At first I was so nervous I couldn't process the information. After the reality hit me, I was relieved and then oddly disappointed." She turned and stole a glance at Cynthia, who watched her intently. "But…it's a good thing. I want to move on in this relationship the right way without the added responsibility of a child that neither of us is prepared for. I have no idea how Claude would have taken the news. He may have done the gentlemanly thing or he may have lost it."

"From everything you've told me about him I don't think he would have lost it."

"You're probably right. But I want him to want me for all the right reasons, not because he feels that he has to."

Cynthia nodded and reached out to cover Melanie's hand with hers. "Well, now you have all the time in the world to find out."

Chapter 19

Melanie returned home feeling lighter and totally positive. She couldn't wait to talk to Claude, hear his voice. She practically skipped through the house as she teased Evan about dinner, begging for just a small sample, to which he resoundingly said no.

Undaunted she went to visit her brother, who informed her that he'd gone for a long walk up and down and up and down the hall. "That nurse is a real tyrant," he'd joked.

Veronica and Jessica were gone for the day but had left her some notes on prospective clients. She was reading them over when she heard the doorbell ring. She frowned. She wasn't expecting anyone and it was too late for any deliveries.

She walked out of her room and went to the top of the stairs just as Evan opened the door. Her heart jumped when Claude looked up at her with a smile that almost resembled relief mixed with the same joy that rushed through her veins. She hurried down the stairs and ran over to him and into his arms.

He covered her face in kisses until their lips met and held and explored. Finally he released her. Her gaze danced over his face following the trail of her hand.

"What are you doing here? I had no idea…"

"I took the last flight out and I have to leave at the crack of dawn to get back in the morning. But I had to see you."

"You're letting out all the cold air, you two," Alan said from the top of the stairs.

They both looked up and laughed like schoolchildren. Melanie pulled Claude inside and shut the door.

"Let me go and chat with Alan and then I can spend all my time with you."

"Go, go. I'll be here."

He kissed her softly, then turned to go upstairs. Moments later she heard the rich hearty laughter of the two most important men in her life. She hummed on her way to the kitchen, and this time she wasn't taking Evan's no for an answer.

She'd arranged a cozy little setting just off the back porch in the enclosed sitting room. Beyond the tempered glass window the outline of the rocky bluffs and the deep-blue horizon made the perfect picture. She lit candles for the centerpiece, and Evan had prepared the rolling cart with their dinner.

Melanie poured Claude a glass of wine, then sat next to him on the brocade sofa. She raised her glass. "To many nights like this."

He tapped his glass to hers. "To us and many nights like this."

She took a sip and studied him over the rim of her glass. "So tell me, what made you fly out here on the spur of the moment?"

"You. I couldn't stop thinking about you. About us. Last night when we talked I felt that something was wrong. I couldn't pin it down and it was driving me crazy. I knew I had to see you and look you in the eye and have you tell me."

"Oh, Claude, everything is fine. Better than fine." She swallowed. "But you were right." She tucked her feet under her and took his hand. Slowly she told him what had happened, her fears, her elation, her disappointment and her acceptance. "It was silly of me not to be more cautious. It's just that's it's been a while for me," she confessed, "and birth control isn't something that I think about."

"I'm just as responsible as you are. I should have known better but the moment…you…I wasn't thinking clearly." He paused. "It would have been all right, you know."

Her gaze jerked to connect with his. "What?"

"It would have been all right. I wouldn't have run." He ran his finger along her cheek. "That's what I really came here to tell you, what I should have told you when we were together."

Her brows drew together. "What is it?"

"I love you, Mel. I love you so much that it aches inside. I want to be with you. I want us to make this work somehow."

Her soul felt like it opened up and the sun came pouring in. Her eyes burned as tears of joy filled them. She threw herself into his arms. "That's what I wanted to tell you!" she cried an instant before her lips met his in a fiery kiss of passion and promise.

They lay together under the full moon that shone in through Melanie's bedroom window, cuddled in each other's arms.

"What time is your flight?" Melanie asked as she listened to the calming beat of his heart.

"Six. I need to be at the airport by five. I have a car coming to pick me up at four."

Melanie turned onto her side and looked down at him. "That only gives us an hour." She reached into her nightstand and pulled out several condoms. She slinked along his body, placing hot kisses on his flesh, using her tongue to tease and titillate. Claude moaned in pleasure as she took her time awakening every nerve ending in his body until he was practically begging her to stop.

She draped her legs on either side of his body and raised up on her knees, placing his relief only teasing inches away. A look of lust darkened her eyes. "Strawberry or cherry?"

He barely made it on time to meet the car as they tiptoed down the stairs, giggling and whispering along the way.

"I'll call you as soon as I get a free minute. My day is packed," he said as he held her for those last few minutes in the doorway.

"I love you," she whispered.

His mouth curved into a soft smile. He leaned down and kissed her as slowly as time would allow. "I love you, too." He turned to leave and in moments, the SUV was gone.

Trancelike, Melanie closed the door and returned to bed. Burrowing under the sheets, she inhaled the scent of him and her early-morning dreams were filled with images of what they'd shared and all that they longed for.

* * *

With the big Labor Day weekend less than a week away, Melanie realized in a panic that she had done little or no shopping. With all that had gone on in her life she'd totally put her holiday shopping on the back burner. It was a TPS tradition to share gifts of thanks for all the hard work they'd done throughout the year. She and Cynthia had agreed to meet and get as much done as their feet and time allowed.

Living by the water could be bitterly cold during winter, but Melanie loved Sag Harbor at this time of year. The former whaling town reminded her of the Hallmark picture postcards, perfect in every detail.

She and Cynthia met at noon in the center of town, both with a list in hand. After several hours they were loaded down with bags and boxes. But Melanie still hadn't found the perfect gift for Claude.

"I have no idea what to get him," she complained, wanting to include him in the family gathering.

"Socks," Cynthia joked as she put her purchases in the trunk of Melanie's car.

"Very funny."

"You still have a few more days. You'll think of something. Come on. I'm beat and starving."

Mildly disappointed, Melanie climbed in the car and pulled off.

Later that evening after wrapping all of her gifts and stacking them in the designated spot under the living room window facing the ocean, she still hadn't figured out what to get for Claude. She wanted it to be special, a reflection of her feelings for him. But what? When they talked that evening late into the night, she was tempted to just come out and ask him, but whatever she decided on she wanted it to be a surprise.

He was telling her about the long hours he'd spent that day and how difficult the months ahead were going to be after the Senate came back from recess.

"I don't know how often I'm going to be able to get away," he finally said. "Maybe every other weekend. At least until we get some of these bills passed."

As she listened, the possibility of seeing less of him seemed inevitable. An idea began to form in her mind. She had the perfect gift.

On the day before Labor Day, or J'Ouvert, the house was filled with family, and the smell of mouthwatering aromas wafted from the kitchen. Music played softly in the background. Everything would be perfect as soon as Claude arrived.

Melanie tried to conceal her anxiety as time ticked by. His plane should have landed more than an hour earlier and she hadn't heard a word from him.

"Looking out of the window isn't going to get him here any sooner," Alan said, coming up behind her.

His recovery had been no less than miraculous. In

the weeks that he'd been home he seemed to really improve. The weight that he'd lost was coming back and his strength was returning. He'd started taking morning walks and had begun exercising again. Every night, Melanie sent up her thanks for healing her brother.

He put his arm around her waist, then leaned down and kissed the top of her head. "He'll be here, relax." He brought her back into the living room where the family was playing a mean game of Scrabble.

Evan came out shortly and announced that dinner was ready. They all filed into the dining room but not before Melanie took one last look out of the window. She saw his Suburban pulling into the driveway, and she nearly screamed with relief and joy. She pulled the door open and ran out to meet him.

The moment he saw her running toward him he knew that the decision he'd made was the right one. He caught her up in his arms and kissed her soundly.

"Now that's the kind of welcome a man can get used to."

"Then get used to it," she said, kissing him again.

"Let's get you inside. Everyone is waiting." He took his two shopping bags of gifts from the passenger seat as they walked together to the house.

Dinner was a loud, laughter-filled affair, typical of Harte gatherings. Stories were shared, lies were told and their unwavering love for each other was renewed.

After they were full and dessert was served, they all tumbled into the living room for more talk and frivolity.

Claude felt totally at home. He'd never experienced this kind of family love. His growing-up years were worlds apart from this. This is what he'd been missing and searching for, waiting for the right time. A home. With people to love and who loved you back. He pulled Melanie close and was happier than ever that he'd found her.

"Okay, I can't wait a minute longer," Jessica announced. "I want to open presents!"

"You don't have to tell me twice," Vincent said, diving toward the stack of gift-wrapped boxes like a five year old.

That was the signal. Everyone joined in, finding a space on the floor, shouting out names on boxes and passing them along to the recipient.

Melanie laughed in delight. This is what it was all about, family and being together with the ones you love.

Claude's heart was racing out of control when Melanie turned to him with a slender white box in her hand topped with a bright red bow.

"For all your hard work," she whispered with a double meaning and held the box out toward him.

He swallowed and picked up the plain white bag near his feet. He took out a box that looked like it could fit a Sunday go-to-meeting hat. He handed it to her.

"Open it."

"Let's open ours together," she said, eager to see the look on his face.

He untied the ribbon and she untied hers. Inside, her box was filled with pink tissue paper. She looked up at him curiously.

"Keep looking," he said.

She pulled the tissue away, and tucked deep inside was another box of white velvet. Her fingers shook as she lifted it from its cushion. Her insides were trembling so badly she could barely get the box open and when she did all the air rushed out of her lungs.

An exquisite diamond sparkled back at her picking up the light from the candles, making it glow even more.

"Oh…Claude…"

The room had gone silent as Claude lifted the ring from its temporary home. He held it out to her.

"I love you, Melanie Harte. More than I can ever explain. And if I know nothing else, I know that I want to spend the rest of my life with you. Will you marry me?"

She blinked several times. She looked at the ring,

at Claude and then at her family, who seemed to hold their collective breath. She turned to Claude.

"Yes, yes, yes, I'll marry you.'"

A whoop of joy shot through the room as her family screamed and hollered.

Claude slid the ring on Melanie's finger and pulled her into his arms. "I love you," he whispered.

She sat back and with tears in her eyes she looked at the diamond on her finger.

"That's what took me so long. The jeweler had to do a last fitting. I thought I was going to lose it while I waited. Are you happy?"

"I can't tell you how happy I am."

With that they were swarmed with kisses and hugs and well wishes.

"I say this deserves a toast," Alan said and began pouring drinks for everyone.

They all held up their glasses. "To my new brother and my amazing sister."

They all toasted the newly engaged couple.

"Open your gift," Melanie said, putting down her drink.

Claude pulled the top off of the box and inside were two plane tickets to Paris. His eyes widened in surprise. "Paris."

"The City of Lights. You said how hard you were working and that this week's break would be the last one for a while. I wanted to make it special. Our plane leaves tomorrow."

He cupped the back of his hand behind her head and pulled her toward him. "It will be the perfect place to *experience* our engagement."

After piling up plates to go, hugs, kisses and well wishes, one by one the family said their goodbyes and headed to their respective homes.

"If you two handsome men will excuse me, I'm going to send Evan home and straighten up the kitchen." She started to get up and Claude pulled her down into his lap, setting off Melanie's giggles.

"What if I don't want you to go?" he said deep into her ear that sent a shiver from the bottom of her stomach right up the center of her body. He nuzzled her neck.

With great reluctance Melanie tore herself away from the cocoon of Claude's arms and went to the kitchen. She blew him a kiss.

"Get a room," Alan teased.

Claude lowered his head and chuckled. "You were right, man."

Alan relaxed against the overstuffed cushions of the couch. He put his feet on the matching ottoman. "I usually am, but what about this time." He reached for his glass of wine.

"About me needing to find someone."

"Yeah, but I didn't think it would be my sister."
He chuckled.

"Are you cool with that?"

Alan leaned forward and rested his arms on his thighs. He looked right at Claude. "I love my sister. All I want is for her to be happy. Since she lost Steven all she's done is pour herself into the business. She'd been so busy putting other people together she put her own life on the back burner. If I could choose anyone for her it would be you."

Claude's lips tightened as he nodded his thanks. "She's some kind of special, man." The awe of it was in his voice. "I mean…from the moment we met. I know that sounds really corny but it's true. I couldn't stop thinking about her."

Alan grinned. "Mel does have that effect on people."

Claude rested his right ankle on his left knee. "Yeah, I thought for a while that something was going on with her and Rafe Lawson."

Alan threw his head back and laughed. "You're kidding. Rafe? Rafe is the poster boy for 'ladies man.' I'm surprised that Bradford was able to wrestle him into agreeing to use the service at all."

"He had his eye on Melanie. No doubt about that."

"As much as Rafe has his eye on any woman. It

was probably her not falling all over him that was the attraction."

"Yeah, I'm sure you're right." He paused for a moment, somewhat reluctant to broach the subject, but he knew Alan would be honest with him. "What was Steven like?"

Alan's brow rose and fell. "Hmm. Steven Ellis was a great guy. No other way to put it. He adored the ground that Mel walked on. He was much older than her. A professor at the college she attended. They met, dated, married and then before we knew what happened he was gone. It was a tough time for all of us. Everything was so hush-hush back then. The stigma. The fear."

A frown of confusion creased his brow. The words rang in his ears. *Stigma. Fear.*

Alan's gaze darted away for a moment. "AIDS-related pneumonia. That was the official diagnosis," he said in a faraway voice. He shook his head in sadness.

The air rushed out of Claude's lungs like he'd been punched in the gut.

"We told everyone it was a heart attack. Back then it just wasn't something that you talked about."

His frown deepened. "But…how?"

"Steven had been in a bad car accident a few years earlier. He'd received a blood transfusion." His silence said the rest.

Claude swallowed. The tightness in his chest cut off his air. He folded his hands on his lap. "My God. And Mel," he looked at his friend with questions and empathy in his eyes.

"Tore her up. For five years she got tested every six months. Then once a year. Miraculously she always came up negative. The doctors cleared her totally about two, maybe three years ago. I think the only people who really know what happened are Steve's family—who sued the hospital for millions—Cynthia and me. The kids have no idea."

Claude drew in a long, shaky breath and slowly exhaled. Why hadn't she told him something like that? Didn't she trust that he would understand? Did she think he would stop caring? She'd lied to him.

"I know what you're thinking. I can tell by the stunned look in your eyes."

Claude's eyes jerked toward Alan. "What?"

"You want to know why she didn't tell you. She will. I know my sister."

Obviously Claude didn't. He didn't know her at all.

Chapter 20

Alan had said his goodnights and gone up to bed. The house was quiet. The night was still. A sprinkling of stars glittered in the night sky. The full moon cast an ethereal glow. Her ring caught the light and sparkled in a burst of color. She smiled as joy took life and ran through her veins. She had never felt so happy or so at peace.

Claude gazed down at Melanie. Her eyes were half closed. He could see the gentle outline of her smile in the muted light. She was happy. He'd done that for her. That was all he wanted to do. He wanted to make her happy and live every day to see the joy in her eyes and on her lips.

That could never happen. Not now. He squeezed his eyes shut as the pain of the unthinkable shot through him. Life without her. After he'd waited so long.

She'd lied to him. He needed to hear her tell him why. Without the truth how could they ever go forward? They would be stuck in this place of distrust that he'd found himself in. They could never build a life together on a foundation of lies.

"Claude…"

The single word was spoken so softly that he thought he imagined it.

"Claude…" She turned slightly toward him.

He opened his eyes and looked down into her upturned face. His heart banged in his chest. She took his hand and held it.

"Can we go for a walk?"

"Now?"

She bobbed her head. "The coastline is incredible. The stars are out. The moon is full. A warm breeze is blowing off the ocean. I want to share that with my husband to be on the first day of our engagement."

His stomach twisted. His heart ached. He touched her cheek. "Sure."

Melanie tucked herself against Claude, resting her head on his shoulder as they walked along the bluff and down toward the shore.

Warm, moist air blew lightly around them, sprinkling them like fairy dust, and Claude silently prayed for a magic wand to make the incredibly devastated feeling that knotted his insides go away. He wanted the conversation with Alan to have never happened. He wanted to turn back the clock. He wanted Melanie to tell him the truth on her own without any prodding from him. It had to come from her or it would never be right again between them. He held her tighter and kissed the top of her head.

"Steven and I used to walk along this path," she said quietly.

Claude's body momentarily stiffened. He barely breathed.

"It was the only thing he looked forward to… toward the end." She paused for what seemed like an eternity and for a while Claude thought she wouldn't say anything else. She would just leave things like that, unfinished and unanswered. But then she spoke and the words, the hurt, the fear, the acceptance flowed from her and into him, joining them in a way that he could not explain.

"I…I thought I would die too when he came home and told me." She hesitated. "He'd been feeling ill, tired. He was looking worn and wasn't eating. I told him he was working too hard and he needed a vacation. He insisted that we would take one as soon as the semester was over."

He felt her body shudder against him as she drew in a breath. He held her a bit tighter.

"I finally convinced him to see a doctor. They started talking about T-cells and life expectancy, experimental treatments, drug cocktails…and our world began to come apart." She swiped at her eyes.

Her anguish was palpable and he couldn't bear to have her relive that heartbreaking time in her life. Not for him. Not even to appease his need to know the truth. It wasn't worth her pain.

He stopped walking and turned her to face him. "You don't have to do this. You don't have to tell me."

"But I do. I should have told you in the beginning, before we slept together. Before we had sex without protection. But I wasn't thinking. I was being selfish and needy. That wasn't fair to you. But I was afraid. I lied. I told you the story we've been telling people for years. Even now, with all the information, the treatments, the miracles and success stories, the fear and stigma still remain." She lowered her head to hide the tears that slid down her cheeks. "I don't think I could have stood to see the look in your eyes."

"Look at me." He lifted her chin and forced her to look into the depths of his love for her. "No matter what life throws at us, we can beat it if we trust each other." His dark eyes moved soothingly across her pained expression. "You have to believe that you can trust me. Trust me with your secrets, your joys, your sorrows, your hopes. And I have to believe that of you. We are putting our lives and our hearts into each other's hands." He cupped her face in his palms. He lowered his head and kissed away her tears, then leaned back.

"The first thought that came into my head wasn't fear for myself but the fear of realizing that you didn't trust me enough to tell me, and it scared me to think that was the way we were going to start off our relationship together—hiding things from each other."

Her throat tightened. "I lived in fear. Month after month. Never knowing if this test result was going to be the one…" She blinked rapidly to stem the flow of tears. Her face squeezed together as she fought them back. "The only thing that held me together after I lost Steven was staying busy and helping other people to find and fall in love. But all the while I wanted what they had." She sighed heavily, turned away from his penetrating eyes and began to walk again.

He moved quietly beside her.

"I dated. But never anything serious." Her smile was rimmed with sadness. "I didn't dare let it go that far. Everyone always wanted to know how I can be so good at what I do and not have a man in my own life." She drew in a long, slow breath. "I could because I

knew what love felt like, what it looked like, what
it was like to hold it in your hand and watch it fly
away." She sniffed. "Finally the doctors gave me a
clean bill of health. I breathed easy for the first time
in years." She gazed up at him. "Then I met you." Her
throat tightened. "I saw possibility again. I wanted a
chance to live and love again." Her shoulders shook
as emotion overtook her.

Claude pulled her into his arms, wrapping her in
his warmth, in the strength of his love. "You don't
have to be afraid of anything. Never, ever again. I
promise you." He lowered his head and kissed her,
slow and sweet, sealing his bargain with her heart.

She melted against him, drawing on his strength,
holding onto the love she held in her heart for him.

"Let's go back," he whispered along her moist
lips. "I want to show you exactly what I'm talking
about."

The moment Melanie's bedroom door shut behind them, Claude began a leisurely exploration
of her body, marking his territory with a touch, a
kiss, a nibble. Nimble fingers unbuttoned the one
closure, and the cream-colored silk and jersey ankle-
length overtop drifted to the floor. The matching
wide-legged, accordion pants and fitted top soon
followed.

Melanie took his hand and guided him into the

bathroom. She turned on the tub, added aromatic bath salts and turned on the jets of the Jacuzzi.

"Let me entertain you," she said, unbuttoning his shirt and freeing him from his slacks.

The mirrored space filled with steam and the heady scent of jasmine and patchouli. They pulled off the rest of their clothing. Their bodies grew moist from the steam.

Melanie pressed her damp body against Claude's and took his growing erection in her hand. Her tongue dipped and teased his right nipple. He groaned deep down in his throat and sucked in air through clenched teeth while her slender fingers encircled him, moving up and down in slow, practiced strokes until he jerked and quivered within her grasp.

An uncontrolled urgency rose up within him and he moved her up against the sweaty black and white wall tiles, lifting her and draping her legs over the bend in his muscular arms.

Her cry became trapped in her throat when Claude's single hard thrust pushed up inside of her, gluing her to the wall, sealing her to him.

She linked her fingers around his neck and buried her head against his chest as he effortlessly lifted her up and down onto his rock-hard shaft even as he stirred his hips in a circular motion, making her dizzy with delight.

She felt the rush of her climax begin to overtake

her. She tried to outrun it, to make it last, but she was losing ground.

"Oh, God, oh God…Cl…oooohh, agggg…"

His palms clasped the firm globes of her behind and he could feel the shivers running through her as her body became a conduit of electricity that he thrust in and out of her. It shook her, stiffened her muscles, coursed through the blood in her veins and she came in strangled, powerful bursts that opened and closed around him in rapid succession until she was limp and trembling.

Through sheer force of will he pulled out of her, his erection jumping in protest at leaving the wet, hot cocoon. He lowered her legs to the floor and she leaned against him.

"I thought this was your show," he teased, leading her, dreamy-eyed to the waiting Jacuzzi. He helped her get in and he followed, both of them sinking into the swirling hot depths.

They sat so that her back was resting against his chest. The steam enveloped them, giving them the sense of being part of a dream.

Melanie closed her eyes, reliving those final seconds before her climax. A shiver ran along her spine. Her clit jumped and throbbed under the water. She moaned softly as Claude cupped her breasts, his thumbs rubbing across her hardened nipples. He played with and caressed them until Melanie swore they would explode. He nibbled the back of her neck and dipped his hands beneath the scented water. He spread her thighs and slid his middle finger up and down her slick folds, dipping in and out of her center.

"Slide down and lean back against me," he instructed. "Spread your legs."

The force of the jets rushed against the hot pulse of her womanhood. A strangled cry shot from her throat. Her head spun. The pleasure was so sudden and so intense that she shook from the force of it, wanting it but fearful of its power.

"Relax." He massaged the inside of her thighs. He took her right leg and draped it over one side of the tub and then did the same thing with the other leg. She whimpered helplessly against the sensations that rocked her.

Claude secured her against him by wrapping one arm tightly around her waist. With his free hand he fingered her, playing along with the force of the water, and her hips began to move. They rose and fell in rhythm to his manipulation of her and the force of the hot pulsing water.

"That's it, baby." He slid a finger inside her and she came hard and fast. "Enjoy it. Ride it." He kissed the back of her neck as her body bucked and she moaned, moaned until there was nothing left but her soft whimpers. "I...I can't wait any longer," he groaned. "I can't…" He gritted his teeth against the need for release that was building inside him like a monsoon ready to hit the shore.

Melanie summoned her last ounce of strength and pulled herself up. She turned around to face him, straddling him. For a tantalizing moment she hovered above his throbbing erection before slowly lowering herself onto him and riding him to ecstasy.

Somehow they managed to untangle themselves, wrap up in towels and tumble into Melanie's bed.

Her limbs ached. Her vagina throbbed. She'd never felt so good and so thoroughly loved in all her life. If this was any indication of what being married to Claude was going to be like, she was definitely going to have to spend more time in the gym. She giggled.

"What's funny?" he murmured against the back of her neck and spooned her closer to him.

"Oh I was just thinking that if I plan to keep up with your sexual acrobatics for the rest of our life together, I was going to have to stay in shape."

"Hmm. My sentiments exactly." He gently squeezed her breast and slid his hand down between her legs. She was already wet and the realization raced through him. She wiggled her behind against him. "Don't start something you're not ready to finish," he warned.

"Who said I wasn't ready?" She covered his hands

with her own, one above and one below and gently guided him to do exactly what she wanted, all the while she erotically rotated her behind against his rising shaft. She pulled his hands away and turned fully onto her stomach. She took two pillows from above her and shoved them under her pelvis and rose up on her knees. She tossed him a come hither look from over her shoulder and that was all the invitation that he needed.

Epilogue

Fortunately, Melanie and Claude's flight to France was scheduled for the evening and they delighted in being able to sleep well past ten in the morning. And they wouldn't have gotten up then if Melanie hadn't scooted away and locked herself in the bathroom, while she laughed hysterically at Claude's baleful pleas of "just one more time."

Laughing until tears were in her eyes, she turned on the shower full blast and after a long, hot, solo shower and darting away from Claude's playful grasp while she got dressed, Melanie took over the kitchen and prepared a lumberjack breakfast for the two most important men in her life.

She wasn't sure this day would ever come around again for her, she thought as she mixed the batter for biscuits and placed the feather-light dough on the baking tray. She took the juicer from the overhead shelf and set it down on the counter. She gazed at her ring. It was all still so surreal. She ran a finger across the perfect surface. But it was real. She was in love and Claude was in love with her. They were engaged and going to be married, and to celebrate that they were going to spend a week in France. She sighed dreamily. Just her and Claude. No worries about running into family members in the hallway or tempering their sounds of passion as they shared and gave love to the fullest.

She'd been to Paris many times before, mostly on business. But this would be the very first time she would experience the great city of love and lights with the man of her dreams. She was giddy with expectant energy and couldn't wait. If she had her way she'd leave right at that moment. And then it hit her.

With Evan off for the day, and Vincent out of town with Cherise, and Victoria and Jessica off doing their thing, Alan would be alone for the night. The first time he'd be entirely alone since he'd come home from the hospital.

She'd been so enmeshed in the drama of her own life, she hadn't bothered to pause and consider her brother. How could she even think about leaving him alone? If something happened she would never forgive herself. She had been the one who insisted that he come and stay with her so that she could take care of him.

She gripped the edge of the counter before shoving the tray of biscuits into the oven. Maybe she could get someone from the rehab center, one of the nurses who'd come when he first came home. She turned the oven on low and darted to her office in search of the number.

Flipping through her electronic contact list she located the number. While she dialed she prayed that someone would be there on Labor Day.

The phone rang and rang until the automated message came on.

"Happy Labor Day. Our office is closed and will re-open on Tuesday. If this is an emergency please hang up and dial 911."

It was an emergency of sorts, but not the kind they meant. Frustrated and with a level of panic beginning to grow she racked her brain for an alternate solution and came up empty.

She should have thought it through instead of being so impulsive. That was so out of character for her. Everything she did was well planned and thought out—except when it came to her and her life. What was she going to do? How was she going to tell

Claude that their romantic getaway would have to be postponed?

Maybe she could call the airline and rearrange their flight. It would cut their time away short but at least it wouldn't be a total wash. Tomorrow, the girls would be back and she was sure they would have no problem staying at the mansion and looking after Alan.

She sniffed the air. The smell of burning bread propelled her out of her seat. She ran down the hall to the kitchen, only to find Alan and Claude already investigating.

They turned almost identical expressions of joviality at her.

"Wow, Evan's gone for one day and our breakfast is shot to hell," Alan teased.

Claude pulled the tray from the oven. Smoke filled the space. He turned on the overhead exhaust fan. "They don't look salvageable, babe," he said. "Hope this isn't an indication of your culinary skills, sweetheart." He winked at her.

Melanie stomped into the room and surveyed her minor disaster. "I got distracted," she offered up as an explanation. She took the oven mitt from Claude and dumped the tray in the garbage. "I'll have breakfast ready shortly, minus the biscuits."

"Are you okay?" Claude asked quietly. "It's really no big deal about the biscuits."

She wished it was that simple. Her gaze darted toward her brother, who was half in and half out of the refrigerator. "I need to talk to you," she mouthed.

Concern drew his brow into a tight line. "Sure." He took her hand and led her out of the kitchen. "What's wrong?" he asked once they were out of earshot of Alan.

She blew out a breath. "I don't know how to tell you this, but we're not going to be able to go to Paris. At least not tonight."

"Did something happen?"

"I was so focused on getting you the perfect gift and us being together that I completely forgot about Alan."

"I'm not understanding. What about Alan?"

"How can I leave him here alone? Sure he's much better, almost his old self, but he had a heart attack. Anything could happen while we're gone. I called the nursing service and no luck. The kids are away and won't be back until tomorrow and—"

He placed his hands on her shoulders. "Baby, it's okay. I understand. I didn't think of it either. We can always go to Paris. Your brother is more important." He pulled her into his arms. "We'll make our own getaway right here," he said softly and kissed the top of her head. "It will be fine."

She looked up at him, doubt swimming in her eyes. "Are you sure?"

"Positive." He smiled. "Seriously."

She breathed a sigh of relief. "Thank you," she whispered.

"For what? For loving a woman who cares about her family?"

She kissed his lips.

"Uhm, uhm."

They turned in the direction of the interruption. Alan was leaning against the door frame.

"Don't you two ever get tired? Maybe I can get some rest tonight. I won't have you both keeping me up all night." He faked a yawn.

Melanie was mortified. Claude burst out laughing. She elbowed him in the side and flashed him a scalding look.

"Whaaat?" he asked innocently.

She rolled her eyes, then focused on her brother. "Well you'll have to get used to it because we're not going."

Alan's head jerked back. "Not going? Why not. I was planning on having the house to myself."

"I can't leave you here alone, Alan. It's too soon."

"You're kidding, right?"

"No, I'm not. Claude and I talked it over. It's settled."

"So a twosome is now a foursome."

"What are you talking about?"

"I'd asked a *friend* to come by and keep me company. I didn't bother to mention it to you since you weren't going to be here anyway."

Melanie folded her arms and lasered in on her big brother. "A friend? What friend?"

"A woman friend, if you must know. And she's very good at taking care of me." He grinned.

"Alan but your heart...the doctors said..."

"The doctors said when I could walk up and down a flight of stairs I had the all clear. I've been doing that for a couple of weeks now...building up the old stamina."

Melanie pursed her lips. "Who is this woman?"

Alan checked his watch. "Well, she should be here around three. You can meet her then."

"Since I didn't know we were going jet-setting I don't have a thing to wear," Claude said in dramatic fashion, throwing his hand over his eyes.

Melanie giggled. "Stick to politics. We can get whatever you don't have when we get there. We'll do the tourist thing." She took her lingerie and tucked them into her suitcase.

Claude came up behind her and peeked over her shoulder. He reached around her and lifted a hot pink thong out of the suitcase. He dangled it from his finger. "I am going to thoroughly enjoy taking this off."

She snatched it away from him and tossed it back into the suitcase. "I'm not going to make it easy. You're going to have to work, baby."

He put his arms around her waist. "I never back down from a challenge."

She turned around into his arms. "My kind of man." She snaked her arms around his neck and kissed him softly on the lips.

The sound of the doorbell filtered upstairs. "Oh, that must be her!" Melanie jumped away and hurried to her bedroom door. She peeked her head out and listened.

"Hey, Lorraine," Alan greeted. He took her overnight bag.

"Her name is Lorraine," Melanie said in a tight whisper.

"I'm sure he'll introduce you if you come out from behind your door and go downstairs," he whispered back.

She huffed and pulled the door open fully. "Come on," she said, grabbing his hand and tugging him along behind her.

They came downstairs as Alan's lady friend was taking a seat on the sofa. She looked like a swimsuit model for *Sports Illustrated*. She was gorgeous and sexy. She would give her brother another heart attack for sure. What was he thinking? Silly question,

Melanie chastised herself. She knew exactly what he was thinking.

Alan turned in their direction. "Mel, Claude. This is Lorraine Hampton. Lorraine, my sister Melanie and her fiancé Claude Montgomery."

Melanie crossed the room with her hand extended. Lorraine stood up. "Nice to meet you, Lorraine." Claude shook her hand, as well. "It's great to know that you'll be here with Alan while we're gone."

"Alan and I go way back. It's not a problem. Thanks for having me in your beautiful home."

Melanie sat down and Claude sat next to her.

"My dear sister is worried about me. So let me cut to the chase. Lorraine is a forensic profiler for the FBI. She's actually the chief of the department."

Melanie fought to keep her mouth from falling open.

"Al told me you manage a very elite dating service."

"Hmm, yes. Along with my two nieces and my nephew."

Lorraine leaned back with a bright smile on her face. "That sounds absolutely fascinating. How does it work?"

Melanie relaxed and told Lorraine about the ins and outs of the business, gave her a brief history and regaled her with some of their success stories. Before long they were laughing and talking like old friends. Melanie found out that Lorraine was not only a forensic profiler but also a professor at Harvard. She continued to dismantle any misconceptions Melanie may have had and, once again, she realized that she had pegged someone wrong.

She thought about it all through the flight to France. But when they arrived and took the rented car to the château that she'd arranged for, she put all thoughts of work and miscues out of her head. This was her and Claude's time and she wasn't going to let anything distract her from pouring all of her attentions on him.

It had been ages since either of them had actually taken a trip that wasn't work related and they totally immersed themselves in doing everything a tourist would do.

Claude was blown away to discover that his lovely fiancée was totally fluent in French as she flawlessly gave drivers directions, ordered meals and read the signs and billboards. He simply relaxed and let his lady take the lead.

During the day they toured the streets, ate breakfast at sidewalk bistros, shopped until they were exhausted, toured the Louvre and the Eiffel Tower, walked along the Seine River and one day they took the Bullet Express and spent the day in Italy.

The nights were reserved for them. The cook that was part of the château package prepared their dinner, served, cleaned up and subtly disappeared. It was during the romantic, quiet times that they talked, sharing childhood stories, books they loved, movies they hated. They talked about politics, religion, the economy and what they hoped and dreamed for the rest of their lives together.

The week seemed to fly by and before they knew it, they were spending their last day in the city of love.

Melanie stepped out onto the terrace of their château. The lights of the city of Paris spanned out before her. She drew her robe around her body and watched the purple sky begin to brighten with the morning sun.

Claude stepped up behind her and wrapped his arms around her waist. Tenderly he kissed the back of her neck.

"It's like a fairy tale," she said softly, nestling into his embrace.

"One that will never end."

"I've been thinking about how we are going to see each other with you in D.C. most of the time and me in Sag Harbor."

"So have I. I'm going to resign."

She spun around. "No."

"I can't ask you to leave what you love. It wouldn't be fair to you. I can work anywhere."

She took his hands. "I've done what I've done for a long time. I've helped hundreds of couples find love. Now I've found mine and I've taught my nieces and nephew everything I know the same way my grandmother and my mother taught me. It's time for me to secure my own happiness, and that's with you. And just as the business was turned over to me, I'll turn it over to them. And the Harte legacy will continue."

He searched her face. "Are you sure?"

"I've never been more certain about anything, except you."

He held her close, reveling in the joy that she brought to his life, and as he kissed her he vowed that he would spend every day of their life together making her happy.

And as Melanie swayed in the arms of her husband to be, she knew that her grandmother and her mother were looking down on her with smiles on their faces. She'd traveled the rainbow in search of the pot of gold and she had found her reward, at last.

* * * * *

REQUEST YOUR FREE BOOKS!

2 FREE NOVELS
PLUS 2 FREE GIFTS!

KIMANI™ ROMANCE

Love's ultimate destination!